"Does anyone think Mr. Carruth and Jake share some resemblance?" Chloe asked

Jake halted, turning to stare at John. His gaze swept John's suit with displeasure. He would never wear his hair that short, either. *"No."*

John considered Jake's dirty jeans, worn-out boots and seen-better-days cowboy hat, under which shoulder-length dark hair flowed. "I have to agree with him."

Cody the clown chuckled. "Twins," he said.

Erin stepped over to Jake, surprising him by sliding off his hat. He let her, smelling the delicious scent of her perfume. "You do have some resemblance," she said. "Mostly around the eyes and chin. And the same hair color, a nice charcoal."

Stunned, Jake stared at John, who glared back at him. It couldn't be. There way. They had n

"So," Cody hire John Carru r to do it than fa

Dear Reader,

I'm so excited to participate in Harlequin American Romance's anniversary celebration. It seems like just yesterday that I wrote my first book for Harlequin American Romance, following in the footsteps of authors I admired, such as Barbara Bretton, Dallas Schulze and many, many others.

My kids were very young, then—babies, really—and now my daughter is in college and my son in high school. I remember meeting the editor who bought my first American Romance book. I had my little daughter with me and my husband, and when I chanced to run into my new editor and was introduced, I was so excited I exclaimed, "Oh, let me hug you for buying my book!" I've published many American Romance novels since that first fortunate sale, and I must say the thrill has never diminished. Over time, the line has evolved and changed, but it still keeps its core of heart, family and touching emotion.

I hope you enjoy celebrating Harlequin American Romance's anniversary with us, the fortunate authors who are privileged to be read by readers like you who have enthusiastically supported our work and loved our stories all these years.

Best wishes,

Tina Leonard

Tina Leonard

THE TEXAS TWINS

featuring

The Billionaire
The Bull Rider

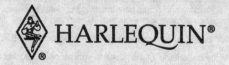

HARLEQUIN®

TORONTO • NEW YORK • LONDON
AMSTERDAM • PARIS • SYDNEY • HAMBURG
STOCKHOLM • ATHENS • TOKYO • MILAN • MADRID
PRAGUE • WARSAW • BUDAPEST • AUCKLAND

Lisa and Dean, I love you. Mumzie.

ISBN-13: 978-0-373-75267-6

THE TEXAS TWINS

Copyright © 2009 by Harlequin Books S.A.

Recycling programs for this product may not exist in your area.

The publisher acknowledges the copyright holder of the individual works as follows:

THE BILLIONAIRE
Copyright © 2009 by Tina Leonard.

THE BULL RIDER
Copyright © 2009 by Tina Leonard.

www.eHarlequin.com

Printed in U.S.A.

CONTENTS

ABOUT THE AUTHOR

Tina Leonard is a bestselling author of more than forty projects, including a popular thirteen-book miniseries for Harlequin American Romance. Her books have made the Waldenbooks, Ingram's and Nielsen BookScan bestseller lists. Tina feels she has been blessed with a fertile imagination and quick typing skills, excellent editors and a family who loves her career. Born on a military base, she lived in many states before eventually marrying the boy who did her crayon printing for her in the first grade. Tina believes happy endings are a wonderful part of a good life. You can visit her at www.tinaleonard.com.

Books by Tina Leonard

HARLEQUIN AMERICAN ROMANCE

986—RANGER'S WILD WOMAN†
989—TEX TIMES TEN†
1018—FANNIN'S FLAME†
1037—NAVARRO OR NOT†
1045—CATCHING CALHOUN†
1053—ARCHER'S ANGELS†
1069—BELONGING TO BANDERA†
1083—CROCKETT'S SEDUCTION†
1107—LAST'S TEMPTATION†
1113—MASON'S MARRIAGE†
1129—MY BABY, MY BRIDE*
1137—THE CHRISTMAS TWINS*
1153—HER SECRET SONS*
1213—TEXAS LULLABY**
1241—THE TEXAS RANGER'S TWINS**
1246—THE SECRET AGENT'S SURPRISES**
1250—THE TRIPLETS' RODEO MAN**

†Cowboys by the Dozen
*The Tulips Saloon
**The Morgan Men

THE BILLIONAIRE

Chapter One

Ruthless. Some said driven. An only child and self-made billionaire, John Carruth liked things his way. The sexy blond woman giving him five feet six inches of attitude clearly had no intention of giving in to his wishes. She stood in front of his desk in his new office, hands on her slender hips.

"Renaming the rodeo isn't a good idea. The people in No Chance, Texas, do things a certain way."

"Let's discuss it over dinner," he suggested. After working with Chloe Winters for two weeks, John knew she wasn't likely to jump at the opportunity. John figured he'd never really had a meaningful relationship, but he'd taken a *lot* of women to dinner. When a man made a lot of money, he had female companionship for the choosing. Ask Donald Trump.

Chloe shook her head, her eyes sparkling with temper and probably a naive assumption that it was inadvisable to mix business and pleasure. In John's opinion, it was always good to mix business and pleasure—it made for more interesting dinner conversation. The lawyer in her no doubt dictated extreme professionalism, and anyway, John could tell from the way she carried herself—with pride and a certain standoffishness—she wouldn't be an easy woman to seduce.

He was sort of glad for that. It was time for him to give up women, maybe until he found "*the* one," or at least someone whom he could regard as "*possibly* the one." In fact, on this beautiful Texas June day, he told himself it was time to turn over a new leaf and take all women seriously before he ended up becoming a schmuck.

"Look, John," Chloe said, "you can't rename the rodeo without speaking to people who have lived here all their lives and believe their town name is part of their identity."

"No Chance is an awkward name. It's not attractive on billboards. Something like Windy Corners has better appeal. We need marketability."

It was probably too late to change the name for this year, anyway. The rodeo was in four weeks. Someone had told him they'd received around twenty rider entries. The name of the rodeo was a millstone dragging down its popularity, as far as he was concerned. He wasn't a romantic or a superstitious person, but what cowboy would want to enter a rodeo called No Chance?

The problem was obvious.

"Just because you have a major ownership stake

in this rodeo doesn't give you the right to romanticize the town to suit your city ways," Chloe told him.

"I promised to give an honest appraisal of how to make this rodeo profitable. In the five years this rodeo has been in existence, it's barely broken even. First thing that needs to change is the name."

"In your opinion."

They were at an impasse. He hadn't officially renamed the rodeo—not yet, anyway—but he'd had a full-color mock-up made of a brochure for when he met with the rodeo committee tomorrow. He'd wanted to test his idea on Chloe first, get her reaction, so he'd know how to sell his idea to the others. Chloe thought the rodeo's old name was appropriate, but he knew it turned off sponsors.

No big-name riders would enter without big-name sponsors. Life was simple when one understood money, and he'd quickly realized from the proposal the town of No Chance had sent asking him to invest in their rodeo that the people here had little understanding of the wonderful, alluring challenge of making money. Thanks to his parents, he understood money very well. Lured like a shark smelling blood, he'd left New York on a whim.

He'd expected resistance to some of his proposed changes. Yet something more romantic and yes, practical, was needed to save this rodeo, something befitting a community that didn't want to change but did want to grow. It was a too-still place, with few amenities. John felt he could change all that if he could work through the issues his way. Wait until they realized he planned to build a huge hotel here, make this backwater into a tourist destination that included an enormous Ferris wheel the size of the London Eye in England, and ultimately gambling casinos to rival those in Las Vegas and nearby Louisiana.

He was going to have to go slowly, but he would attain his goals in No Chance. The sweet sound of ka-ching! would have to serve as his applause. He doubted the good citizens would appreciate his plans for their downtrodden town, where the only plant had long since closed. Apparently, No Chance's paper plant had been run out of business by the neighboring town of Farmbluff. Feelings were still running hot about that, though ten years had passed.

Miss Ice Cool, with her smooth blond hair and constant opinions, saw herself as No Chance's protector. She was determined to thwart him, question his every move. And since she was the town's legal counsel, he put up with her debating. Truthfully, if he needed to boot any of the lawyers he had working for him, he'd consider hiring her. Chloe was tenacious and persistent, traits he admired in a tough lawyer. She could sway the close-knit coterie of the town council his way if she chose to, so he needed her support.

Chloe supported nothing but the side she was on. John tried his winning smile on her. "You and I have got to work together better."

"I have no problem working with you."

"Working *against* me."

"Your words, not mine." She glanced down at her notepad, marshaling her next argument.

He sighed. "I have to consider the bottom line. If the rodeo is going to become the staple of this town, the town may have to consider a name change."

Chloe shrugged. "Good luck with that. I certainly appreciate your efforts to better our situation. But I hope you won't mind me saying that our positions come with a certain amount of conflict built in. You'll find most of us here a stubborn breed."

He raised his hand. "I know, I know—you do everything your way. And yet, the town came to me to finance the rodeo. My opinions come with the deep pockets."

"We were hoping for a more silent hero."

"You and I will probably argue a lot," he warned.

"Not me. I'm all about peace and quiet."

"Sure, sure." John wondered if she allowed anyone a peaceful moment.

"So," Chloe said, "let's get back to this brochure—"

One of the rodeo clowns—a beloved stalwart of No Chance—rushed into the room. "Chloe," he said, "we've got a problem."

"Calm down, Cody," she said, reaching out to soothe the elderly gentleman. "What is it?"

He glanced at John. The billionaire was considered very much an outsider; no one was sure what to make of him. Some people said he was cold, too business-like. Others liked him, thought he was working hard to improve matters, had a strong guiding hand which had been sorely lacking in the town's business matters before. Chloe respected John. He was a smart man, but he was too handsome, too magnetic and too self-assured for her taste. John was tempting as sin and happily arrogant.

"It's okay," Chloe reassured Cody. "What's up?"

"Jessup's here, causing a ruckus. He's telling everyone that our rodeo will never take off because Farmbluff's already setting one up. Got a backing of two million dollars, he claims, from the old coot who owns the paper plant. Some of our boys are about to give Jessup a bit of a lesson he won't soon forget." He glanced at John, not certain if he should continue. "The sheriff's on his way."

"I'll go," Chloe told John, but he followed her out of his office and down the narrow aisle as Cody hurried off.

"This type of thing won't help the rodeo," John observed, and over her shoulder Chloe sent him a look of pure annoyance. "Bad reputations are hard to change. This is the third fight we've had here this week, and it's not good for the town's reputation."

"Do you ever think of anything besides the bottom line?" Chloe demanded.

John shook his head and kept walking.

JAKE FITZGERALD saw that the visiting cowboy was more than drunk. He looked a bit crazy, but that was nothing new for Jessup. It was a warm day, maybe already ninety-seven degrees by the noon hour. Everything was melting in the heat, yet Jessup was still spoiling for a fight. Jake watched as the ever-efficient Erin O'Donovan peered at Jessup lurching down the walkway between the stalls. He'd known Erin since first grade. For some reason she'd moved to Farmbluff six months ago, a mistake in his opinion, but there was no stopping Erin once she got an idea in her head. There never had been. She'd been first in all their classes, gone off to study medicine at Columbia, grabbed a few scholarships. Erin was a whirlwind of activity, and Jake had always had a secret yen for her.

He was a bull rider, always on the circuit. He had nothing to offer a petite high-energy redhead. At the age of thirty-two, he had almost nothing to offer anyone. A saddle, a truck, some riding equipment, a hundred acres south of town. He looked at her legs beneath her emerald-green skirt, and with a certain hunger he had no intention of satisfying admired the way her white blouse skimmed her curves. Gentle Dr. Erin, committed to patching up cowboys at rodeos. Thing about Erin was, despite moving to the enemy town, she'd never forgotten where her real friends were. She came back all the time to check on them, most particularly Cody and his dicky heart.

Erin could check on *his* heart any time.

"Jake," Erin said, startling him. "Have you met the new rodeo director and general partner, John Carruth?"

He put his hand out to the suit-wearing city slicker. "We've spoken once. Welcome."

John shook his hand. Neither of them were very

warm about the encounter. Chloe had preceded John into the enclosure to look at Jessup and she sent Jake a brief smile. He nodded, then went back to perusing Erin. Something possessive he hadn't expected reared up inside him insisting he somehow make certain the new Rodeo Savior in town didn't get an itch for Erin.

They watched the drunk cowboy shadow-box a few circles, jabbing at the air occasionally, doing himself more damage than anyone else. Cody put a hand on the cowboy's shoulder to calm him, then jumped back when an errant swing whizzed by his ear.

The sheriff spoke up. "Mr. Carruth, you're probably the one who should decide if you want to press charges of any nature. Maybe Jessup just needs a nice, comfy jail cell until he cools down"

"Well, Counselor?" John said. "Would you advise that?"

"I suppose he really needs a safe place to sleep it off," Chloe said.

Sheriff Whitmore nodded. "We might see if we like him any better when he dries out, Mr. Carruth."

"Please, call me John."

Jake bet the man had probably said that a hundred times since he'd come to town. He was trying hard to fit in—everyone said so. Yet no one really seemed to warm up to him.

"I'd say the show's over," Sheriff Whitmore said. "Deputy Gonzalez, cuff our visitor, please."

Chloe frowned. "Did anybody ask him why he thinks our rodeo is destined to fail?"

"It is," Jessup said, whirling to face her. "Farm-bluff already has all the best names lined up. I just came by to tell you not to waste your time." He tipped to the left, putting himself out of reach of Deputy Gonzalez's cuffs, then righted himself. This whole drama was typical bad behavior for Jessup, nothing new, but John Carruth stood awkwardly in a corner, looking uncomfortable and out of place in his suit. He didn't seem to know what to think about small-town intrigues.

Jake caught John staring at Chloe, who didn't seem to notice the man's attention. It would be amusing to watch Mr. Suit try his city-slicker skills on Chloe. Chloe was married to her horse, like any good barrel rider.

"Chloe, weren't you here since about four this morning working Brandy?" Sheriff Whitmore asked.

"Yes." Chloe sank down on a concrete block next to Erin. "John was here, too."

All heads turned to stare at the outsider with the stiff suit and the rare smile. John shrugged. "Work-aholic, what can I say?"

"I never saw Jessup, though," Chloe added. "I don't think anybody in No Chance would serve him so much liquor."

Sheriff Whitmore scratched his head under his straw Resistol hat. "Jessup, you didn't need to come here and tell us y'all's rodeo is better than ours," he said as Deputy Gonzalez finally succeeded in cuffing the man, earning more curses from the drunk cowboy. Jake decided to go do something productive and leave the rodeo politics to Mr. Suit. It'd be a great initiation for him. Personally, Jake thought it was dumb that the man was brought here in the first place. All No Chance wanted from John was his wallet; he could have sent his money and stayed in Manhattan.

"Does anyone think Mr. Carruth and Jake share a resemblance?" Chloe asked suddenly. Even Jessup stopped fighting as all the occupants of the crowded breezeway glanced at Chloe, then John. "It's just unusual to see two men who are the same height, dark-haired, square-jawed, each with really blue eyes," she pointed out.

Jake halted, turning to stare at John. His gaze swept John's suit with displeasure. He would never wear his hair that short, either—almost military-style. *"No."*

John considered Jake's dirty jeans, worn-out boots, and seen-better-days cowboy hat under which shoulder-length dark hair flowed. "I have to agree with him."

Cody the clown chuckled. "Twins," he said.

Everyone laughed at the absurdity of that statement. Erin stepped over to Jake, surprising him by sliding off his hat. He let her, smelling her perfume and the delicious scent of warm, clean Erin.

"You do have some resemblance," she said. "Mostly around the eyes and chin. And the same hair color, a nice charcoal." She slipped his hat back into place and stepped away—he'd been electrified the second she'd moved so close to him. His throat was dry; his blood beat hard.

If he wasn't careful, he was going to blow his cover where Erin was concerned. Jake forced his mind back to the businessman. John's expression was ill-disguised distaste. Jake shrugged, unable to blame him. "It's a small town. Everybody always thinks everyone is related to somebody."

"I see." John slid his gaze over to Sheriff Whitmore who was deep in conversation with his deputy. "Do you need anything from me, Sheriff? I have a conference call in fifteen minutes."

Cody laughed again. They were all used to Cody's humor—he was a great clown, enjoying life more than the average inhabitant of No Chance. Too old for real "bullfighting" now, Cody kept audiences entertained between riders.

"Marjorie had twins," Cody said. "She sent one out of state to her sister's to be raised, and kept Jake here. That's why she married Bert Fitzgerald, to cover the whole thing up. 'Course Bert didn't care. He knew he couldn't have children of his own, and he'd always loved Marjorie."

Stunned, Jake stared at John, who glared back at him. It couldn't be. There was no possible way. They had nothing in common. Nothing. And who the hell was their real father?

"So," Cody said, "that's why I suggested we hire John Carruth to save our rodeo. Who better to do it than family?"

Chapter Two

John sat in his office, reeling. He'd stared at Cody after his announcement, felt his heart drop to his shoes as he glanced at Jake, who didn't seem any happier than he was with the news. Then he'd stalked off to the protective walls of his office and slammed the door. It wasn't possible. He did *not* have a brother. John's brain whirled, his temper rising. Cody was the one who had sent John the original offer about the rodeo. It hadn't had the ring of huge money to it, and there was no guarantee he would have pulled No Chance's rodeo proposal from the pile of portfolios and brochures he received. There hadn't even been the usual phone call to push the presentation for No Chance. The proposal hadn't been that slick or professional.

Yet, John had been drawn to it, recognizing that a part of him yearned for this type of adventure in his life.

Now he was just plain mad. If there had been a family connection, it should have been made plain in the proposal. This smacked of conflict of interest, if Cody was telling the truth.

John took a deep breath to calm himself. There was absolutely no way. Cody had him confused with someone else. The startled astonishment on Jake's face had shown he had no prior knowledge of Cody's outrageous claim.

John had grown up far away from here, enjoying private schools and sophisticated circles of family friends. Privileged beyond compare, he'd experienced love so giving that he still missed his parents every day. They had instilled in him his work ethic and a concern for those less fortunate. His glittering world would seem like outer space to the people of No Chance.

He and Jake could not be more different.

He ignored a knock on his door. This was his office, damn it. The small-town people who were proud of knowing everybody's business could just butt out. At the moment he was ticked, and he had no plans to be unticked anytime soon.

He hadn't said "come in," yet, the door opened. Stunned, annoyed, he waited. Chloe poked her head around the door to look at him. "Excuse me, but I got voted the designated buttinski. I'm to make certain you're not about to do something—or most particularly yourself—any harm."

Erin's head appeared next to Chloe's. "Me, too. Well, she drew the short straw, but I'm here for moral support in case you don't take kindly to being checked on."

He could do worse than have two attractive women looking in on him. John rolled his eyes, sending a message that he was disgruntled so that he could keep the all-important barrier up between him and *them*—the busybody townspeople quickly scripting themselves to run his life. He was not going to be the affable Jimmy Stewart, whose life was taken over by sweet, determined small-town denizens. Jimmy's character always learned a lesson in his movies. John was proud that he always outsmarted the lesson before he had to learn it.

He waved a hand impatiently at Erin and Chloe. "Come in and shut the damn door," he said, injecting plenty of crossness into his tone.

"My, you are a bear," Chloe said, leaning against the edge of his desk instead of taking one of the nice, rickety wooden stools that served as office furniture for now. "That was kind of a shock, I guess, so you're forgiven."

He looked up at her, glanced at Erin who was busily trying to lock the door, which, as he'd learned to his chagrin, had a handle that malfunctioned. "Leave it, Erin," he said. "It probably hasn't been more than an ornament for the past twenty years."

"The rodeo is relatively new," Erin said.

"But the grounds are falling down," he replied crossly. "Let's just call the doorknob small-town charming and forget about it."

"Okay," she said, taking the stool that Chloe had declined. "No conference call?"

"No." He'd used the excuse so he could leave the gathering. Erin probably suspected he'd been fibbing, but at this moment, he wasn't exactly the biggest fibber in this town so he didn't care. "I suppose you all knew."

Chloe shook her head. "We had no idea."

"Jake isn't any happier than you are," Erin said, her tone conveying an edge that caught John's attention. He looked at the redhead with interest as he pulled a bottle of Crown Royal whiskey from his desk, along with a six-ounce crystal glass.

"John!" both women exclaimed at once.

He glanced up at Chloe. "What?"

"You drink!" Chloe exclaimed.

John poured himself a generous shot. "Sorry. I should have offered you a drink, ladies. Care for one?"

"This is a dry county," Chloe told him. "Sort of the buckle on the Bible belt."

"I know it's dry," John said, pulling the drawer open so she could peer inside it. Three nice bottles of Crown Royal sat hidden in their purple-wrapped, lovely packaging—his very own ammunition against incidents just as these. "No worries. I was forewarned so I stocked up before I arrived."

Chloe blinked. "Do you drink often?"

"No." He slammed the drawer. "Look. You church-lady types don't have to worry about my soul. It's black. If it was a steak, it'd be burnt. Let's all drink to brotherhood."

Chloe and Erin watched as he knocked back the whiskey.

"Ah," he said, enjoying his sudden role as scoundrel, "tasty stuff."

"I want a glass," Chloe said, and Erin nodded her head.

"Me, too."

He sternly eyed his visitors. "Why?"

"It's not supposed to be good for you to drink alone. So we'll drink with you," Erin said, her tone patient.

"No," he said, "it's *very* good for me to drink alone. In fact, I wish I was alone right at this moment." He gave them both a meaningful glare, but it seemed to bounce right off his uninvited visitors.

"Fill 'er up," Chloe commanded, and John sighed. He usually stopped at one, but with the day he was having, maybe he could stand just a small token shot more.

He filled the glass halfway full. "Help yourself."

"I should think so," Chloe said. "It's rude to eat or drink in front of company." She sniffed at the glass. "This smells lovely."

"Well, be careful. It's not called firewater for nothing." In his old life where he had a penthouse suite and an office that was huge and intimidating, no one would have dared perch on his mahogany desk. No one would have entered without waiting for his command to do so. Familiarity of this nature would have drawn a firing. People respected his ability to make money, but that respect had a healthy dose of fear attached to it, which he'd encouraged with silence and little friendliness.

He watched Chloe take a swig of the whiskey, cough, sputter, and finally burp as she choked.

Patting her back, he took the glass away from her, waiting until she'd caught her breath.

"That's nasty," she said. Her voice was pitched and thin now. "I think my grandmother used to give me that for cough syrup when I was a child."

"Good for granny."

Erin wrinkled her nose. "We just came to sit with you in your hour of need. But I think I'll go see if I can find Jake."

"He said something about Farmbluff," Chloe said, her voice sounding better. "I thought that's what I heard."

John frowned. "He wouldn't pick a fight over there, would he?"

"No." Erin shook her head. "Jake doesn't fight. And our visitor is locked up for the moment until he feels better and is safe for the roads. I don't know why Jake would go to Farmbluff."

John shook his head. "He'll be back soon enough." His gaze slid over Chloe, watching as she pulled her hair up into a ponytail thing. He decided he admired long, lean blondes who burped without shame.

Another knock rapped at the door. "What?" John demanded, cross again. Cody poked his head in and John sighed. "I have not called a town hall meeting in my office."

"I know." Cody looked troubled. "I just wanted to say I didn't mean to spring that on you like I did. I've never been known for being delicate."

"Good to know," John said, "although a little late for the warning."

"Yeah," Cody said, "life sometimes sucks that way. Okay, I'm going back to do my job. Glad you're all right. Erin, can I have a word with you?"

"Sure." She got up and followed Cody out.

The door closed. John eyed the half-full crystal glass, decided it wouldn't help. He caught Chloe staring at him.

"What?"

"You don't have as bad a temper as I thought you would."

"Rage isn't what the situation calls for, is it?"

"I don't know." She stretched long legs, looked down at him. "What does it call for?"

"More whiskey." But he didn't pick up his glass.

"Do you want me to leave you alone?"

He met her gaze, shrugged. "Not really."

"So, tell me about this desk," Chloe said. "Somebody forgot to tell you what a rodeo office looked like?"

"This was my celebration purchase when I made my first million."

She raised a blond brow. "Something special about a desk?"

"I like the feel of wood." He ran his hands over the gleaming top, caressing the smooth, masculine architecture of the mahogany. "It feels powerful, strong and permanent."

But nothing was permanent, so that was a dumb sentiment. He'd thought he had the most sane, organized childhood, segueing into adulthood without a hitch. Everything about his life was clearly a lie, and yet, it was almost impossible to be angry with his parents. They'd made him the center of their universe. His father had died, and then his mother, both of them letting him know on their deathbeds that he had been a perfect son to them. He could forgive them for not telling him he was adopted. In their minds, they had been his only family, and perhaps he loved them even more for that. "I think I'm going to head over to the B and B and call it a night. Mrs. Tucker will be surprised to see me so early," John said, capping the whiskey and putting it away.

Chloe nodded, saying nothing. She stood, walked to the door before looking over her shoulder at him. "Good luck."

"Yeah. Thanks." She had a great fanny, packed into worn jeans. He supposed it didn't matter since she wasn't likely to let him near her wonderfully heart-shaped fanny. He considered his options of the moment. He didn't like to be lonely. At least not tonight. Female companionship was preferable to sitting around stewing over his newfound sibling and the trick—yes, he called it a trick, a sleight-of-hand—that Cody had pulled on him. There were too many questions he wanted to avoid, too many raw emotions he needed several days to process before he felt anything but anger. "Or I could invite myself over to your place."

Chloe shrugged, delicate shoulders moving beneath her pink T-shirt. "You could."

"Chloe, may I come to your house for dinner? If I bring steak and maybe a good red wine?"

She looked at him for a long second. "Just bring yourself. That will be fine."

She left, closing the door softly behind her. John swallowed. Just bring himself? He didn't know who he was anymore. Who was John Carruth? Not the man he'd thought he was this morning.

"What the hell," he said, finishing the glass of whiskey. He didn't necessarily want more. For a few seconds, he debated what he did want, and then decided there was no putting off the inevitable.

He went to find Cody.

JOHN FOUND Cody staring at the "guest of honor" in the two-room jail cell on No Chance's main strip. The strip consisted of twenty stores and restaurants, all old and usually empty except for locals visiting one another. It was the hotbed of activity, and as far away from life in Manhattan as John could imagine.

He sat down in a chair to listen to Cody and the sheriff chat with their guest. They glanced at him but without much more than a nod his way. John wondered if he was finally beginning to fit into the fabric of No Chance.

"It's your rodeo, Mr. Carruth," Sheriff Whitmore told him. "You wanna ask the questions?"

"Call me John," he said for the hundredth time. "I'll just listen to you for now. Listening's my favorite sport."

They went back to perusing their guest, who lay flat-out on a bed, his hat over his face.

"Tell us the true purpose of your visit here," the sheriff said, and Jessup pulled his hat off his face, spat on the floor, then replaced his hat.

"I'll bet," Cody said, "that you can probably keep him here overnight on a charge of public intoxication, right, Sheriff?"

"Intoxication," Sheriff Whitmore corrected. "I could, but I don't care to. I'd rather send him on his way once he's sober. I just want to know a little more about what our visitor wants here."

"I want my lawyer," the cowboy said, and Cody laughed.

"Who's your lawyer?"

"Chloe Winters," the cowboy said.

The men stared at him.

"How could that be?" Cody asked.

The cowboy sat up. "Because I know she's a good lawyer. And I know she'd be on my side because I've done nothing wrong."

"It's true, technically," John said. "He's done nothing wrong. He's a minor annoyance, beyond the public drunkenness. Of course explaining yourself a bit more would be helpful," John said, "and since you're here warning us that Farmbluff is setting themselves up to compete with us, you clearly want us to know."

"Just feel sorry for you." The cowboy lay back down, staring at the ceiling. "You'll find it hard to book sponsors and riders. We've got all the best lined up."

"And there's not enough to go around?" John asked curiously.

"Not with towns thirty minutes apart," the cowboy said.

"Ah. Good point." John decided to keep working the cowboy, now that he'd decided to open up. "So if you were in my shoes, as owner of this broken-down rodeo, what would you do?"

The cowboy was silent. Sheriff Whitmore glanced at John. Cody shrugged.

"Okay." John stood. "Hey, I've got a date, so I'm going to head out."

"A date?" Cody straightened. "Who's the lucky lady?"

"Not that kind of date," John said, hoping it actually was. "I should have called it a casual meeting of friends."

The cowboy sniffed. "Good luck, if it's with Chloe."

"Really?" John's brows raised. "Any particular reason?"

"Nah. Not unless you like man traps."

Sheriff Whitmore and Cody both stared at the cowboy.

"What the hell does that mean?" Cody demanded. "Other than you're just begging for an ass-whupping."

"Don't get crazy, clown," the cowboy said. "You're not the only one keeping secrets around here, and if you're not careful, some more ugly things will come out tonight."

"Now, look," Sheriff Whitmore said, and John walked to the bars to stare at the cowboy.

"What is a man trap?" he demanded. "Buddy to buddy, give me a little advice, since you're a guy who likes to pass along a warning."

"All the guys dig Chloe," the cowboy said, "and absolutely no one gets past hello."

"She wouldn't give you the time of day," Cody said.

The cowboy sat up. "Hey, Cody, don't you think it's about time you go see your brother?"

"You shut the hell up," Cody commanded, suddenly tense.

"Surprise," the visitor told John. "Farmbluff's best clown is Clem the Bad, Cody's brother. Bet he didn't tell you that, City."

Cody blinked. "I have no brother."

"Yeah, well, lie as you like. If you ever decide to own up to it, and to why Clem might be determined to see your rodeo fail, tell 'em Jessup Bratton sent you." Jessup laughed. "How does it feel to have all your dirty laundry out for everyone to see, Cody? I just couldn't let you get by with lying to this dime-store cowboy without takin' a little revenge on you." He winked at John. "Cody acts harmless, but he and his brother are mean as snakes. Don't be fooled, friend. That's my final word of wisdom to you."

John stared at Cody. The clown's face turned red. It was true, John realized. Cody did have a brother with whom he shared bad blood, and who obviously was out to destroy No Chance's rodeo. This fact hadn't been included in the proposal and literature Cody had sent him.

But then, he hadn't known that Chloe was the local "man trap," either, and he wasn't sure which piece of news he found most disturbing.

Chapter Three

At midnight, Chloe realized John wasn't going to show. He hadn't called to cancel, either, and it would have been a simple matter for him to ask someone for her phone number. She blew out the candles in the dining room and turned off the jazz CD. "Inconsiderate lout," she muttered, "typical male."

A sudden knock on the front door startled a squeak out of her. "Who is it?"

"A very late dinner date," John replied.

She opened the door, curious to hear his excuse. "Have trouble finding my house?"

"No." John held out a box of microwave popcorn and a bottle of wine. "Peace offering?"

"Maybe," she said. "Come in and I'll decide after I hear your excuse." He didn't appear to have been hitting the whiskey again, so Chloe felt hopeful that if he'd gotten cold feet about visiting her, perhaps they'd warmed back up again.

"I should have called," John said. "I had to escort the prisoner back to Farmbluff."

"Why?" Chloe went into the kitchen, taking out two wineglasses. She passed an opener to John, allowing him to do the manly duty of uncorking the wine. "Do you want popcorn now?"

"Not exactly. I had a burger on the way, my treat for Jessup, who was starved after ranting all day. The popcorn was the only edible thing I could find at the gas station when I filled up. Not exactly what I would normally bring." John slid the cork out of the bottle. "His motorcycle wouldn't start. I borrowed the sheriff's truck to haul it back, and then had to go switch it out for my car when I got back."

"Any reason you didn't tell Jessup to have one of his Farmbluff buddies come get him?"

John grinned. "There's probably no better way to get information out of a man than to sit him in a confined truck cab and ply him with food and more liquor."

"Dirty pool," Chloe murmured, admiring how sexy John looked despite the fact that his suit was now rumpled. "Have you ever considered purchasing a pair of Wranglers?"

"Yes," John said, "first thing tomorrow, I'm buying a truck and some jeans. If things are going to get down and dirty around here, I need to dress for the occasion."

He followed Chloe to sit on the sofa. "What's going to be down and dirty?" she asked.

"Well, for instance, Cody has a brother in Farmbluff he didn't tell me about."

Chloe's brows raised. "Clem the Bad." She slid

her feet underneath her and sipped her wine. "Everybody knows."

"I didn't."

She shrugged. "You can't know everything."

"Did you know Clem was trying to torpedo No Chance's rodeo?"

"No," Chloe admitted. "I never knew Farmbluff was interested in having their own rodeo. I thought it was the paper plant owner pushing for it."

"Okay. So Cody's innocent on that."

"I don't know," Chloe said. As handsome as she found John, he was an outsider. This was her town, her friends, her family. John would leave one day—this rodeo thing was just a play toy for him, a fleeting boy's dream, no doubt. As soon as he realized it was hard work and disappointment and dirt, flies and heat, he'd head back to Manhattan. Likely he'd never think about her once his heels cleared the town. "Cody's clever. That's all I'll say. And," she said, "Cody's my father."

John stared at her. "Are you serious?"

"You'll note the intelligent genes." She smiled at him. "You might say we're two of a kind, peas in a pod."

John laughed. "You're pulling my leg."

"No," she said solemnly, shaking her head, "you had noticed we both have the last name of Winters?"

"It hadn't crossed my mind, but now that it has, I guess I'll…have to be nicer to the old fellow."

She smiled. "That's not what you're thinking at all. So anyway, go easy on Cody when you get steamed up about the Clem-the-Bad connection. He's my uncle, after all."

"Close family?"

"Not particularly." She wasn't going into any more detail; she'd shared enough about her family tree.

"So," John said after a long moment, "the next thing I learned is that you have a reputation that is quite at odds with what I know about you."

"Really?" Chloe considered the sexy businessman, admiring his blue eyes, dark hair, devil-may-care smile. Had he always been able to acquire everything he ever wanted in his life? Of course he had.

Until he came to No Chance and restarted his life, she supposed.

"You're quite the ice maiden," John told her with a wink, "according to Jessup Bratton."

"That's my reputation?"

"Yes."

Chloe put her glass down. "That's fine by me. Especially if Jessup says so."

He laughed. "I suspected as much."

"You don't think it's true."

"Men who gossip about a beautiful woman usually got turned down."

She looked at him. "Do you want me to pop that popcorn?"

He laughed. "No, thanks. I'm going to go. This is a late Friday night for this city dweller. I've kept you up long enough."

She had a hot guy in her living room, one who was unattached and not looking for a long-term relationship—and he was leaving. Obviously he'd had second thoughts about what he'd come for—and she could put that down to finding out about Cody. But blood was thicker than anything John had to offer. She'd felt his annoyance with Cody and hadn't wanted John to criticize him, not that he didn't deserve some criticism. But he was her father. Now John was looking for an out; she could provide one. "Yes, you have kept me up quite late. I get up early in the mornings."

He laughed again, and pulled her into his arms. "I figured you'd be a challenge."

He kissed her, and Chloe's head spun as he worked his charm on her, taking advantage of her surprise. He smelled wonderful, she realized, and had strong fingers, a warm chest…something wasn't right here. "Wait," she said, and he pulled away from her.

"Wait?" he asked.

She nodded, knowing she was crazy to let him out of her arms.

"Did I cross a line?"

"No." She didn't want to melt this fast for him. What good would it do? This hunk of a guy would leave her heartbroken as soon as he realized he wasn't cut out for a small, dusty town far away from the creature comforts he seemed to enjoy. They had nothing in common.

He stood, leaned down to give her a less simmering kiss than the one that had threatened to undo her resolve a moment ago. "You'd be much nicer to sleep with than Mrs. Tucker over at the B and B."

He surprised her. Maybe he didn't care that she and Cody were family. Still, she wasn't jumping into the fire. "But she makes breakfast, and I don't."

"Fair enough." Heading to the front door, he turned and looked at her. "Could you tell me where Jake lives?"

"Paying another late-night visit?" She wondered why he suddenly wanted to know after seemingly avoiding all thoughts of his newly discovered twin.

"I might."

She hesitated. "Do you want company?"

"Sure. Lead the way."

JOHN RAPPED on Jake's door. The small farmhouse was dark, no surprise since it was so late. He had the urge to see his twin, get to know him. Decide if they had anything in common. Would they be as awkward a fit as Cody and Chloe seemed to him?

One thing they didn't share was obvious: John was an insomniac, and clearly Jake was a heavy sleeper. John pounded on the door, annoyed that no lights flipped on. "Jake!"

"He's not here," a female voice said in the darkness.

"Erin!" Chloe explained.

"Yes. It's me."

"What are you doing?" John demanded. She seemed to be sitting on some sort of porch swing, so he clarified, "Sitting in the dark by yourself?"

"I was looking for him, too." She sniffled, and he realized she'd been crying.

"What's going on?" he asked.

"He's gone," Erin said. "He left a note on the door for the mailman."

Only in a small town could a note be left on a front door concerning mail.

"He said he was going to Farmbluff, didn't he? That doesn't rate a note on the door to the mailman," Chloe said.

"The note says he doesn't know when he'll be back."

Chloe went to sit beside Erin, so John followed. The swing creaked under their weight. "Because of me," he said.

"That's my guess."

"The proverbial 'this town isn't big enough for the both of us.' Maybe Cody should have left me living my lonely life."

"I doubt you were lonely," Erin said.

No, but finding out he had a family member had given John an anchor he hadn't realized he'd been missing. "I always wished I had a sibling."

"Did you?" Chloe asked.

"Yeah. My parents—I guess my adoptive parents—always told me they couldn't have more children. What I never suspected was that they hadn't even had me." He'd delve into that later. Right now, he just wanted to figure out how he fit into No Chance. "Hey, isn't Farmbluff your stomping ground?"

"Yes, but Jake doesn't belong in Farmbluff," Erin said.

"That's true," Chloe agreed. "I'm up for a road trip if we decide to drag him back where he belongs."

"I'm heading off," Erin said. "You two can linger on Mr. Fitzgerald's porch, but I've said my good-byes."

Erin walked off the porch, got in her car drove away.

"No point hanging around here," John said.

Chloe could tell he was somewhat sad that Jake had gone. Together they walked to his car, getting in silently, and then Chloe shocked him by leaning over to kiss him. He waited, letting her lead the way, and when she didn't pull back, John realized he was getting a new signal from her. Rumors, all rumors, this business of Chloe being icy. He started the engine, slowly driving away from Jake's house, and meandered up the road to Chloe's, giving her plenty of time. When he finally made it there in slow motion, he shut off the car and reached for her, his heart pounding.

Chloe gasped.

"What?" he asked, and then he heard it, too.

"Roam, roam on the range!"

John wondered what lonely, horny cowboy lay in wait for Chloe. "Who is it?"

"It's Cody!" Chloe hopped out of the truck. John followed her, wincing at the sound of drunken howling.

"Where never is home, a discouraging gnome!" Cody bawled from his prone position on the porch,

and then bellowed in a great crescendo, *"An' the pies are not muddy all day!"*

"Dad!" Chloe exclaimed. "What are you doing?"

John followed, bemused. It seemed so improbable that the beautiful barrel-riding lawyer would have any genes of Cody's. "I'm going to need an org chart to keep up with all the family relationships in No Chance," he muttered.

"Where did you get liquor?" Chloe demanded, helping her father to a sitting position. "You haven't touched any since Mom died."

"In his desh," Cody said, waving an arm at John.

John blinked. "You went into my desk?" His private sanctuary? The refuge he'd had carefully carted from Manhattan?

"*I* didn't," Cody said, his slurred voice soft now, conspiratorial. "*Thieves* did."

"Thieves apparently didn't make off with the whiskey," Chloe said sternly. "Come inside, Cody, you're going to wake the neighbors."

"Uh-uh, no, I won't," Cody said. "He had pretty purple boxes with gold crowns on them, Chloe, and I just couldn't help myself."

The Crown Royal box was a thing of beauty. At least Cody had appreciated what he was stealing. John could almost forgive him since the liquor apparently hadn't been wasted on someone who would just as soon drink beer.

"Why do you keep that stuff in your desk?" Chloe snapped, helping her father into the house.

"Because Mrs. Tucker said no alcohol on the

premises, and I didn't want to get kicked out of the nicest—and only—boardinghouse in No Chance," John said. "It was *my* desk, and it was locked, though I don't feel quite gentlemanly pointing that out at the moment."

"You're right. I'm sorry." Chloe gently tugged her father to the sofa. John stood by, feeling helpless, not sure if he should intrude on the family moment. "Dad, why were you stealing John's liquor?"

"I told you," Cody said, squinting, "there were thieves."

"Yes, but did anybody steal except you?" She applied the cold cloth that John gave her to Cody's forehead.

"Yesh," Cody said importantly, "but the sheriff and I don't know who."

Chloe sighed. "Why didn't you call John on his cell phone?"

"We did. He didn't pick up. We figured it was turned off," Cody said defensively.

John started. He *had* switched off his phone when he'd arrived at Chloe's earlier. He'd been hoping to get lucky, hadn't he? No reason to risk interruption. Yet Fate had saved him. He was a big believer in Fate, and angels on his shoulder. He slid a glance to Chloe, reassessing whether he would ever be able to date a woman who claimed Cody as a father. Maybe he'd been saved from himself.

No. He'd take her in spite of the faulty genes. She was sexy as hell. Long-limbed, gorgeous, a challenge in boots... Once he got over the shock, he'd be okay with it. John sat in a flowered chair across from Cody. The clown's eyes were glazed, his white hair wild puffs around his head.

"You think I'm as bad as my brother, Clem," Cody told John. "I've always been proud of not being Cody the Bad."

"Well, when you quit stealing, you can go back to being Cody the Good," Chloe told her father.

"No harm was done," John said, taking pity on Cody, who seemed embarrassed and dispirited. He couldn't bear to see the old man so low.

"You won't be happy…when you see your desk," Cody said, letting out a giant grunt as he relaxed into the yellow cotton pillow.

"Did you have anything important in it?" Chloe asked.

"Nothing but some photos, and the mock-up I'd had made that I was planning to present to the committee tomorrow—"

"Call Sheriff Whitmore," she suggested.

John got to his feet. "I'll just head over and check out the damage myself."

Chloe nodded, glancing at her father. "I'm so sorry about the whiskey. And the damage. If you let me know the extent—"

Cody raised his head. "What are you doing here?" he demanded of John. "You're not—" he hiccupped. "—dating my daughter, are you?"

"No," John said hurriedly. "I don't think so, sir."

"Good." Cody fell back against the pillow again. "Didn't bring no durn fancy-pants city-boy millionaire here to romance my only…child." He coughed, hiccupped and perhaps even farted—definitely farted. Cody had missed a few zeroes in his calculation of John's net worth but he'd gotten his message across: Cody wasn't on board for John as anything more than a wealthy investor in No Chance.

"Goodnight, Mr. Winters," John said softly. "Goodnight, Chloe." He left, not sure what else to say.

Fate had indeed saved him.

Chapter Four

John's desk was a shambles. Drawers were pulled out onto the floor, the neatly organized papers scattered. Strangely, whoever had paid him a visit hadn't had a taste for expensive whiskey. Except for the liberal helping that Cody had sneaked, the rest of it was untouched.

The mock-up was gone, which he'd expected. He knew more now than when he'd accepted this challenge. There was bad blood between people, family relations and two towns, and he was caught squarely in the middle. He and the few million dollars he'd sunk into this venture.

He wanted to wring Cody's scrawny neck, which would do no good. He'd been thinking of the rodeo only, not calculating the emotions and human drama into the cost.

That was John's job. "And it's starting to add up," he told his desk, annoyed to see a careless scratch here and a scar there that his visitors had left in their hurried search. "There's a good chance I'm in over my head."

Corporate business games were clearly not played with the same skills that small towns used. John felt his blood begin to simmer. First of all, someone wanted to make him look stupid. Second, they clearly thought they could get away with it. He needed to adapt to a different set of skills if he didn't want the rodeo to be a loss on his balance sheet.

Smart businessmen knew when it was time to cut their losses. He thought about kissing Chloe, considered her father's feelings about him. He should know when to cut his losses there, too, but maybe he didn't.

He went home to the boardinghouse in low spirits, cheering a bit when he found a note on his door that there were "milk and cookies in the kitchen." He didn't want any right now, but it was nice to be reminded that small-town friendliness was one of the reasons he'd wanted to undertake this venture. It felt great to take off the rumpled suit—just as soon as he had time to buy jeans, he was never wearing another one, at least not as long as he lived in this town.

For a few hours he slept fitfully, the destruction of his desk and the stolen plans nagging at his sleep. So he got up, snagged a bagel from Mrs. Tucker, who seemed disappointed that she couldn't talk him into hot eggs and bacon, and headed back to the rodeo grounds.

The mess hadn't gotten better. In fact, at five in the morning, maybe it even looked worse.

"Ouch," Chloe said from behind him. "Somebody definitely wanted something you had."

He turned to look at her. "You're here early."

She shrugged. "Brandy and I are always here at five. And I wanted to check on the damage."

She looked good, even at this hour. Long silvery-blond hair up in a ponytail, no makeup, wide hazel eyes totally awake. It was so hard for him to imagine how Cody had managed to create such a vision of a woman—John couldn't even imagine Cody hooking up with a lady pretty enough to create a confection like Chloe. "How's Cody?"

"Sleeping it off." She went in to look at the long scratch on the top of his desk. "You know who can fix this back up as good as new, don't you?"

"I wish I did."

"Cody. He's great with wood. A miracle worker."

John rubbed his chin, wondered if he believed her. What was Chloe's definition of miracle? He wasn't certain the desk would ever be the same. "Why do you call your father Cody?"

She glanced at him, surprised. "He's Cody the Clown. I never knew him as anything different. Nobody ever called him Mr. Winters until you did."

He digested that silently, realizing Chloe's world was vastly different from anything he could possibly understand.

"I like the casual look you're sporting," she said, and he knew she was teasing him. He'd foregone a tie and jacket, dressing down to mere slacks and a long-sleeve shirt.

"I plan to swing by the store today to pick up some new duds."

"Try Belle's Bottoms," she said airily. "Good luck."

She left. John blinked, feeling somehow dismissed. Wasn't she supposed to mention last night in some way? About how disappointed she was that their make-out session was interrupted? About how she hoped she didn't have to wait too long to pick up where they'd left off?

John wondered if he might have imagined her desire for him. He didn't think so. He'd wanted her—still did.

She'd definitely just blown him off, though.

He rolled up his sleeves and began filing papers back into drawers.

"DO YOU THINK he can do it?" Erin asked Chloe as she saddled Brandy. "It's an awful lot to ask an out-of-towner to rescue something he has no emotional stake in."

Chloe wasn't certain. It looked as if the odds were stacked against John. "Dad's usually right about a lot, but this time, even I have my doubts. John and Jake didn't exactly warm to each other. And I don't know how much faith I have in a man who doesn't even own a pair of jeans. I've heard that it takes a unique skill-set to be a successful CEO, and that kind of person can be a CEO of any kind of company, whether it's about making golf balls or widgets. They understand the people component, and the money angle. In this case, though," Chloe said, frowning, "our CEO doesn't even like to get his hands dirty."

Erin brushed Brandy while Chloe checked the horse's hooves. "Jake called me."

"He did?"

"Mmm. Said he'd rented a place in Farmbluff. Didn't even have to pay much rent—when folks heard he was there, they found a place for him to stay."

"Poor Cody," Chloe said, "he really blew it this time."

"I think Jake's been looking for an excuse to leave for a while. Maybe he never really recognized that he wanted to, but John being here gave him the excuse to do it."

"I don't care if he's happy," Chloe said. "Farmbluff is still trying to poach our cowboy."

Erin stopped brushing, walked around to look at Chloe. "What do you mean?"

"Well, they are. Otherwise, why else would they find Jake a place to live? They figure they've got the rodeo all sewn up, now they just need our best attraction. Our star."

"You're right," Erin said, "but Jake would never ride for Farmbluff. He's an independent. He has enough sponsorships to survive even when he's not at his top form."

"That doesn't mean they won't try to convince him. And if the sponsorship had enough money involved in it—"

"Don't even mention it," Erin said. "No Chance needs our finest cowboys or we'll look bad, like we're just a fake wannabe rodeo."

Chloe shook her head. "I'll let his brother worry about him."

She felt a disloyal stab of anger toward her father. If he hadn't meddled, if he hadn't thought he was doing the right thing by bringing John and Jake together, maybe No Chance would still be the happy community it had always been. Now Jake was gone and Cody was tippling again, something he hadn't done in the many years since his wife had died. Chloe had no desire to revisit those painful days of her father's drinking. All this needed to get straightened out—fast. "Move back to No Chance," she told Erin, "we need to keep as many of us here as we can."

"I know. But everybody has to spread their wings sometime. Frankly, I've long wondered what it would be like to live in the north. Or maybe the deep south. There's so much I haven't done." She smiled at Chloe. "Now seems like the perfect time to see what I can do with myself."

But there's no place like home. Did she still believe that? Chloe wasn't certain that she did. Even she was starting to feel stifled by the close-knit community she had always loved.

"At least you'll have your wealthy businessman for a while," Erin said.

"He's not mine," Chloe said. "Cody says I'd be setting myself up for heartbreak, and I know he's right. When a man has dated women around the world much more sophisticated and wealthy than myself—" She shook her head. "Dad advises me to put as much distance between John and me as I possibly can."

Erin swatted at a fly. "Cody wants John to save the rodeo but not date his daughter?"

"I suppose so."

Neither of them mentioned it, but Chloe knew Erin was thinking about Chloe's ex-husband, Bill Wilder. He'd been a good-looking rodeo cowboy, with charm to spare. Chloe had fallen head over heels, faster than a horse throwing her. Bill had hung around long enough to eat some wedding cake before moving on to greener pastures, always following the circuit and sleeping with any woman who smiled at him. The divorce had been painful, a low point in Chloe's life. She'd learned a lot about handsome men who lived on smooth.

Chloe patted Brandy, her stalwart friend. "Dad is usually right about people," she murmured.

"I hope you at least kissed John, if for no other reason than for all that world experience your dad's worried about."

Chloe didn't say anything.

"SO MY PLAN WAS," John said to the three elderly gentlemen and one elderly lady sitting around his office giving him polite stares, "to change the name of the rodeo to make it more palatable."

The town council sat silent, courteously stone-faced.

"See, No Chance spooks off the more superstitious of the cowboys. We derive income from entry fees, but if we don't get entrants, we don't get sponsorship fees. We don't get tourists if we don't get the big-name cowboys. It's a vicious cycle."

"Cowboys can be superstitious, sometimes, like any athlete, or people in general," Mrs. Tucker agreed. "But we like our town name being included in the rodeo name. No Chance doesn't give us the sense of foreboding that it seems to bring to you."

John hardly wanted to argue with sweet Mrs. Tucker who left him cookies and milk at night. Plus, he was going against town pride, a powerful force.

Mr. Pickle, Mr. Hill and Dr. Lambert looked away, their lack of eye contact bespeaking their acquiescence to Mrs. Tucker's words. John wished he had his mock-up and the rest of his presentation; it was hard to deliver a sales pitch without props. He felt their lack of interest and their judgment that he was too green to know what the hell he was doing. "Is there anything I can do to convince you to try it my way?"

"I don't think so," Mrs. Tucker said, "seeing as you haven't even tried it our way yet."

"Haste makes waste," Mr. Pickle said. His straw cowboy hat was torn in places. "We've put five years into this, we feel a year of you researching exactly what it is we've done wrong would be better than implementing a bunch of ideas we're not sure you can adapt here."

"We risk the loss of forward progress for a year and therefore a further financial drain," John pointed out. "Farmbluff already has a full roster of cowboys. It's hard to build this rodeo on the circuit as a viable attraction without a deep commitment from sponsors."

"We know, son," Dr. Lambert said, standing. "You've already run us through all the facts and figures. You'll work it out eventually." He smiled, his bushy long mane as wild as Grizzly Adams's. "We have some faith in Cody letting you buy our gig."

The town council filed out, each man sending a last glance at his wide mahogany desk. Mrs. Tucker clucked at him. "You be sure to get home early for a hot supper, John. I've got it in the slow-cooker for you."

"Thank you." He didn't need to get home early for dinner like a child. He needed to work on this rodeo, which was starting to look like his worst business venture yet. Nobody around here was willing to listen to anything.

He grabbed the briefcase he kept locked in his black Mercedes. If he hadn't been showing Chloe the mock-up, it would still be safely inside the briefcase, safely inside the locked car. But he'd wanted to test his idea on her first, bragging a bit because he thought he'd cleverly get the small town of provincial folks to fall in with his bright idea.

He needed some advice, and probably the best advice he could get was from a rodeo cowboy— even better if it were one who had a stake in the rodeo itself. John wondered whether Jake was in a talking mood, if he could find him.

Still, no one knew the town's history and its people better than Cody, and by extension, his daughter. Now that John had been shot down by the town council, he needed to eat some humble pie.

Chloe had warned him, and she'd been right.

IT TOOK two days for John to run Chloe down. If he hadn't known better, he'd think she was avoiding him.

His first warning sign: she'd changed the time she worked out with Brandy. For as long as he'd been in No Chance, five o'clock had been Chloe-and-Brandy time. How did he know this? He'd been spying. Oh, yes, from the moment he'd first seen the tall, model-like barrel rider, his attention had been caught. There was plenty of room upstairs in the arena, behind glass, where he could watch her. Coffee cup in hand, he'd stood watching—okay, gawking—while she worked with her horse. He hadn't known much about her, but it seemed to him that being around her was a great reason to stay in No Chance.

She was free. Unspoiled, dynamic, spirited—he'd recognized in her everything he could never be, even if he could ride a horse.

Which he couldn't. So he really got a thrill out of watching her.

John could remember seeing ponies in a parade one time when he was a child. When he'd told his parents that he wanted to learn to ride, they'd taken him to a polo club. It was their intention to allow their son to learn the sport of polo, but that wasn't what he'd wanted at all. The smacking of the ball, the flailing of the mallets, seemed much more violent than he wanted. And so he'd told his parents that he'd changed his mind.

Now he understood that he'd never really gotten over the instant love he'd felt for horses. Polo had made him nervous; he would never have played the sport well for fear of injuring the horse. But what Chloe did, racing like the wind, her horse part of a beautiful ballet—that was the magic he'd been craving.

He finally "ran" into her in Brandy's stall, where he'd practically camped out. He and Brandy had been through a bag of carrots while he'd hoped to catch Chloe. "Hi," he said.

"Hello," she said, eyeing the empty bag. "Sneaking treats to my horse?"

"We've been sharing them."

She hung up a bridle, glanced at him. "Nice jeans."

"Thanks. Got them at Belle's Bottoms."

Chloe didn't reply.

"How's your father?"

"Ready to forget the other night ever happened." She wouldn't look directly at him.

"Hey, if it bothers you, I promise not to give Brandy any more carrots."

She shrugged. "John, listen—" Turning finally to face him, she said, "You're a really nice guy—"

Now he felt more than a pinch of concern. "But we can just be friends?"

She looked into his eyes. "That about sums it up."

He couldn't have written a worse script for himself. The script would be titled *Loser Guy* or something crappy like that. He took a deep breath, hiding his disappointment. "All right," he said, "no reason to get worked up over a kiss."

"I agree." She turned away.

"If you don't mind," he said, stuffing the empty carrot bag into his pocket, feeling foolish that he'd ever tried to get to Chloe through her horse when it was obvious that Chloe had no interest in him whatsoever, "I could use your advice on the town council."

She sat down on a hay bale across from him. "If I have any, which I probably don't."

"You're in a unique position to know them well. What they really want. How I can best convince them to see my side of things. You and your father are well-liked, respected. These are attributes I don't necessarily bring as an outsider."

"That's not completely true," Chloe said, "everybody likes you."

"Thank you," he said, keeping his tone business-like, "however, I do hear a *but*."

"The only *but* is that we don't exactly trust that you know anything about what you're doing. It's hard for us to trust anyone who knows nothing about rodeo."

He heard the *us,* the proverbial *we*, and knew he was onto something. Chloe knew the heartbeat of No Chance. "Why did they invite me to take over the rodeo? Are you saying No Chance just wanted my money and not my business expertise?"

"Cody—Dad—clearly felt that…family would care enough about the rodeo to work harder for it." She looked at him. "I suppose that's not really honest, either, because you didn't know you were family. Cody was manipulating you, and I'm not proud of that."

"Manipulating me? How?" To understand No Chance, he had to understand so many people, so many levels of thought. Maybe he'd never learn it all. But he could trust Chloe to be honest with him, insomuch as she understood her own father's motivation.

"To be honest," she said softly, "at first I was afraid that Dad was going to make some terribly dramatic announcement."

"If you don't mind me saying so, the fact that I had a secret brother and parents I didn't know about was pretty dramatic for me." John's tone was grim, perhaps even edgy. And he realized in that moment that he'd been holding in a lot of anger toward Cody. A lot of anger toward life for holding out a game-changer when he was thirty-two. Damn it, it felt like a really awkward time in his life to start over and reassess who he was.

"I'm sorry," Chloe said quickly, briefly lowering her eyes. "I'm being selfish. The first thought that came to my mind was that—I mean, the other night, when Dad found that you'd been visiting me, he wasn't happy."

"I know. I heard."

"And I was afraid that he was going to blurt out

something awful, like you know, he was yours and Jake's real father."

John blinked. Oh, yeah, that would have been bad. He left the words unsaid—the thought had never occurred to him. "I suppose you mentioned that to Cody."

"Absolutely. But he said he was telling the truth about who your parents are."

John nodded. "I've already had a friend of mine verify what your father was saying about my parents."

Chloe looked at him. "Private detective?"

"Something like that." John waved a hand at her. "So, you're giving me the friends-only treatment because your dad doesn't want me dating you."

She straightened. "Don't make it sound like I don't have a mind of my own."

He held up his hands. "I didn't. I'm just curious as to his reasons."

Chloe studied him. "Cody feels that you'll leave No Chance eventually."

"If I have a brother here, wouldn't I be more inclined to hang around? I assume you're saying that your father is beginning to feel that I can't save the rodeo. I'm too green."

"Not necessarily," Chloe said. "I think we're all beginning to feel a little stressed by everything Farmbluff is throwing our way. Like we were outgunned from the start and didn't realize it."

"And you have little faith in me." John didn't really appreciate that. He wasn't the spineless city boy Team No Chance seemed to think he was.

"You just don't understand what you're up against."

John laughed. "Lady, you haven't got the first clue who I am."

"Oh?" She gave him an arch look. "Are you saying that this is nothing? That you could save our rinky-dink rodeo in your sleep? Make a few phone calls, dial up a few friends with connections, and snap! We're profitable?"

He looked at her, considering her words, her proud tone. He saw in her everything he believed was important in a woman: loyalty, faith, commitment.

None of those emotions were for him.

He wanted the same look in her eyes that Erin had when she looked at Jake. Hell, the one overriding thought that had come to him lately was that his country bumpkin of a brother—had he even made amends with the reality that he had a secret brother yet?—seemed to inspire more admiration in people than he did.

John was successful—his bank balances said so—and yet this brother who was his flesh and blood, who had shared a womb with him, seemed to be successful on a scale John had not reached.

He didn't think he liked Jake all that much. That bit of competitive self-pity darkened his already moody soul. Here he'd been avoiding turning into a characterless human by coming to No Chance, doing a deal that wasn't about money but about people, damn it. And he'd run smack into his better half, the saintly, tough, admirable side of the dizygotic pregnancy—Jake. All the good stuff had gone Jake's way, and the Clem-the-Bad kind of genes had leached John's way.

Maybe I should have bought the black hat Belle said would look just right on me. But I wanted straw, trying to look like I fit in around Podunkville. Because all of a sudden I had a yearning to "belong," since I'd just found out my whole life was a lie. I don't know my real parents, but Jake knows them. He was the chosen one, the one not given away.

"I think how Cody lured you here was a mistake," Chloe said softly. "But how long can you go on ignoring your own brother? How can you say you're one of us, when you won't even try to find out what it's like to live in No Chance?"

She probably had a point—did, in fact, have a point, but John wasn't in the mood for good points. He grasped Brandy's bridle so he wouldn't startle the horse, grabbed hold of Brandy's mistress and kissed her, tasting her, before he released her. Then he grabbed up his new cowboy hat, slamming it on his head, angry with Chloe, angry with himself. He'd wanted Chloe to notice he was trying to be one of "them." Hell, "bottoms" wasn't all Belle sold, and he'd allowed her to retool most parts of his wardrobe. He was pretty proud of his new boots as well. Yet in Chloe's eyes, he was just playing dress-up. She watched him, her large eyes full of some silent emotion. Impatient with the unplanned turn of events that were changing him from the person he'd been just a month ago, he gave Brandy a last pat and departed. The horse whinnied at him, but Chloe remained silent.

If Chloe wanted space, he'd give her all she could stand.

Chapter Five

John found Jake the next day, just where the shopkeeper in Farmbluff said he'd find him. Unaware of
who John was, the shopkeeper had bragged about the
champion bull rider they'd snagged from the next
town over. John took mental notes on small-town
rivalry, factoring the information into his game plan.
"Getting much work done?" John asked, coming up
on Jake as he was pulling on riding chaps.

Jake grunted. "What the hell are you doing here?"

Dust twinkled in the still air that hung in the barn,
barely stirred by a wall fan. John couldn't see that
Farmbluff had so much going for it. The town was
the same size, essentially, as No Chance, and it
lacked the camaraderie—at least it seemed so far—
that he was used to in his adoptive town. "Was I
supposed to say, 'Howdy, bro?'"

Jake shook his head. "Let's not wear the brother
thing out, okay?"

John slid onto a rail, noticing how his new boots
hooked nicely over the bottom rung. He was begin-

ning to get this whole cowboy get-up thing. Western wear was functional and it cost nowhere near a Brooks Brothers suit, or a Burberry coat and tie. "I just figured we should talk."

"Haven't in thirty-two years."

"That's true." John nodded, admiring his brother's James Dean-style attitude. Jake didn't owe anybody anything; he lived his life his way. John wondered if he could say the same about himself. "I'm not going to get this rodeo figured out for No Chance without help."

Jake looked at him silently, threw a saddle over the back of a black-and-white horse that John instantly coveted. It was a beautiful creature, long-limbed, graceful, patient. Its mane was black as night, and flipped with attitude when John reached out a hand to touch the curious nose stuck out to him. "So, you're the one person who probably has advice I can really use."

"When did that lightning bolt hit you?"

"Not sure," John said, unfazed by the sarcasm.

"What exactly do you want from me?"

"A partnership," John said honestly. "I really want this to work."

"Why do you care?"

"I care," John said with a sigh, "because I've sunk a lot of money into this venture."

"Bull," Jake said, "otherwise you'd have some of your rich buddies invest in it, fill up the audience with well-heeled cronies, throw a charity ball as the icing on the cake."

"That actually isn't a bad idea."

Jake tossed a glance at him. "What?"

John waved a hand. "The charity ball, etc., etc."

"So do it." Jake sounded like he couldn't care less.

"But there's the human element necessary to succeed," John said. "I need good will to get everybody in No Chance on board with new ideas. The town council feels I need a year to get seasoned."

"What does that have to do with me?" Jake swung up into the saddle.

"Since you're the homeboy, the 'good' brother," John said, thinking of Cody and his brother Clem, "folks will listen to you."

"I live here now," Jake said stiffly.

"Yeah, but you're on the wrong team for the wrong reasons." John slid off the rail and leaned against it. "I'm no reason to leave the town you love."

Jake's blue eyes blazed. "It's none of your business."

"True," John said, "but I need you. You may not need me, but I sure could use the help to save this rodeo. And you want that, too."

Jake leaned back. "So you're suggesting that you're the money and I'm the brains."

"Basically." John didn't mind the insult.

"All right." Jake took a deep breath. "First, forget changing the name. It's stupid. You're stepping on their pride, and they're not going to listen to you."

John already had that much figured out. "Okay."

"I'd quit trying to be an active partner. They don't really want to change."

John looked at his brother, impressed by how fast he cut to the chase. "I'd sensed that."

Jake nodded. "What else?"

"Your friends, not mine, are important to the success," John said softly.

Jake frowned. "Meaning?"

"Aren't a lot of the rodeo cowboys men you've known for a long time?" John asked.

"All my life."

"Then figure out what you need to bring them on board," John said. "I wonder why you haven't sold your own town to them before. Loyalty should be your guide. Why let Farmbluff steal your buddies away from your town?"

Jake looked at him silently, considering his words. "You're saying that riders would be loyal to me."

"Especially if they knew it was to help a cause."

"And you want me to apply pressure on them to—"

"I want you to invite them," John snapped. "Quit being afraid to ask for help. It's not a hand-out. Think of it as inviting your friends to one kick-ass party. Then ask them to *come*."

His brother's eyes darkened. "If they'd wanted to, they would have. Entry forms are there for the taking."

John shrugged. "Everybody wants to feel wanted, Jake." Turning, he walked into the sunlight, heading to his Mercedes. Today, he planned to get that new truck. He wasn't leaving No Chance any time soon, he decided, and he was going to need a proper vehicle.

"Hey!"

He turned to look at his brother. "Yes?"

Jake stopped two feet away from John. "I don't need a brother."

"So?"

"I don't think you're right. In fact, you're dead wrong. It ticks me off that you're trying to make me your party coordinator. This isn't some jet-set event where you send out an engraved invitation and people show up, happy to spend their dough."

"Why not? Farmbluff seems to be doing just that."

"Farmbluff is sponsoring riders. The prize money is huge."

John looked at his brother. "No Chance will have equal or better financial backing."

"Where in the hell would No Chance get that kind of money?"

"Bake sales," John said, annoyed. "Raffles. Church garage sales. Little old ladies' coin purses." He took a deep breath. "I'll provide the financial backing, you get busy inviting your rodeo friends to participate. There's not enough time to do sponsorships this year. But I'll make sure there's enough prize money to make Farmbluff look like a county fair. You bring 'em in, and I'll give you twenty percent of whatever profit the rodeo makes over the next three years."

Jake's expression didn't change. "I don't need your money."

John shrugged. "Never let pride stand in the way of personal success, Jake. Give me more ideas."

"I'll think about it," Jake said, his tone suddenly sharp. "What's it like to be able to buy people?"

John hadn't expected bitterness from his brother. Weren't they on the same team? "What's it like to know who your parents were? To know that they loved you and wanted you?" John shot back.

For the first time in his life, John wanted to take a swing at someone. Jake glared at him, the feeling clearly mutual. This was bad. He couldn't harm the one person on this earth who was his flesh and blood. "Here's a suggestion—get back to No Chance where you belong. I'm no happier about you than you are about me, but being a disloyal jackass isn't going to do anything but make you miserable. Trust me, I know something about this." John got into his Mercedes, peeled out of the dirt-packed parking area, plumes of dust following him as he left. He didn't want to be the bad guy—but it was hard being the good guy, too.

ONE WEEK LATER, some things had changed. John had changed. He now sat at his desk with the door open, instead of closed, in an effort to encourage a literal "open-door policy." If the townspeople had no faith in him, he wanted them to feel right at home coming in and saying so.

Which they did, fairly often.

Jake had not moved back to No Chance, but Erin had, much to his surprise. She said she needed to keep a closer eye on Cody's heart and on a few of her other elderly patients, but John thought he detected a small fib in the redhead's excuse. No Chance might not be big enough for him and Jake, but apparently Farmbluff wasn't big enough for Jake and Erin. He'd never seen two people like each other so much and avoid the love so heartily.

Chloe walked in and laid a stack of envelopes on his desk. For the past three days, she'd done this same thing, brought him unopened mail. It was a new routine for both of them. He hadn't had much to open in the month he'd been here, but suddenly entries were pouring in, maybe ten a day, a lot for a struggling rodeo.

Chloe never said anything other than "There's the mail," when she left him the stack. John watched her, listened for her typical announcement, and told himself that eventually, he would win that barrel racer's heart.

A man had to be patient about sneaking up on people who really didn't want their minds changed about anything.

"There's the mail," Chloe said, turning to leave.

"Wait," John said, surprised by the size of the stack. "How many are there?"

"Sixty," she said. "I told you the rodeo didn't need to change its name. We're going to do just fine."

He didn't tell her that he'd hired Jake to be the rodeo's salesman. Clearly, Jake had a lot of friends. "You don't have to bring me the mail every day. I can get it myself."

"It's sorted about the time I'm through schooling Brandy. It's no trouble to bring it."

He looked forward to her daily visit, but he wanted her to come see him with or without mail. "You changed Brandy's work-out time."

"It's quieter in the arena at night now. And cooler."

She avoided his gaze. John knew she was working out about the time he headed home to Mrs. Tucker every day. Other than delivering the mail, Chloe kept a very low profile. He couldn't call it playing hard to get. It was more like impossible to get. "What would it take to get your father to change his mind about me?"

"Cody likes you fine." Chloe looked at him.

John waved his hand toward the entries. "Besides the fact that Cody and the rest of you think I'm the not-too-bright guy with the money you need, I'm aware that Cody also feels like you going out with me would be very bad karma."

"We don't worry too much about karma here, if you haven't noticed. We're not superstitious, either."

"And yet, your father dislikes the thought of me courting you," John pointed out. "I believe his words were something like 'no fancy-pants millionaire is going to date my daughter.'"

Chloe shrugged. "Cody's harmless, unless you're in the ring with a bull."

"I'm not talking about Cody the clown, I'm talking about Cody the *father*."

"John, if I wanted to accept a date with you, I

would," Chloe said, "whether my father approved or not. I'm a big girl, in case you hadn't noticed."

"I noticed," he said, scratching his head, not liking her answer. "I was hoping that you were avoiding me because your father disapproves of me. I really didn't want to consider that you were avoiding me for your own reasons."

"I'm a professional. My personal feelings about you don't get in the way of wanting this rodeo to succeed. I bring you the mail every day," she said, "so that you don't have to leave this empty box of an office where you hide."

She was sending him a couple of messages. "My door is open so anyone can come in now, even though none of you have ever respected the sanctity of it being closed. How am I hiding?"

"You should be learning to ride. Visiting with the cowboys. Learning what their job entails so you can understand what you're doing."

He leaned back in his chair. "Thirty percent of my time is spent on the phone soliciting donors, managing ads and tracking down the maintenance list for this joint, which is no easy feat. It's damn hard to get a simple lightbulb changed around here, never mind getting a fan rewired."

"Cody does all the repairs."

"I know!" John smacked a hand lightly on his desk. "And he protested me hiring anyone to help him. Yet nothing is getting done very quickly. We do have a rodeo to put on in two weeks, and you want me out there?"

"Cody's just trying to save the rodeo some money by doing everything himself," Chloe said defensively. "You can change lightbulbs, too."

He sighed. "I can. But I didn't hire a secretary to save money this year. I didn't want to add on a bunch of office staff in a year when we weren't figuring to break even. I don't have time to change lightbulbs."

"Cody will get to everything on the list before the rodeo."

John wished he could be so sure. In his big office in Manhattan, people had respected him. He'd never even had to ask for a lightbulb to be changed. No one wanted him to have to ask; even coffee was quietly placed at his elbow every morning, at the temperature he preferred. "That's it," John said. "The problem here is that I'm doing all the changing, and you folks are doing all the squawking."

"Pardon me?" Chloe crossed her arms, her temper starting to rise, John noticed with interest. He wondered about the whole Chloe-the-man-trap thing again and decided life was for the brave.

"That's right," John said. "I've been polite, trying not to step on anyone's toes, but it's time for me to stop worrying about you No Chance folks and your never-ending advice and start paying attention to my investment. I've sunk a lot of money into this venture, and all you residents do is complain and sing the praises of the old days. Well, everything changes today. Right *now*. I can't coddle the sweet apple-dumpling-faced busybodies of this town any longer."

She wrinkled her nose. "You're going to upset people."

"Good." Let her put that in her little stovepipe and just smoke away, or whatever the colloquialism was. "Please close the door on your way out."

She gave him one last glare and left in a visually pleasing swirl of heart-shaped denim-covered fanny. John picked up his silver letter opener and began opening the entries, humming a country song while he considered whose feathers it would be most satisfying to ruffle next.

Chapter Six

Maybe he'd never seen a small-town rodeo, but Chloe watched with a certain amount of fascination as John took to forming No Chance's big event with bullheaded determination. It was almost as though John was daring the rodeo to fail.

It wasn't making him a lot of friends.

He barked orders at extra maintenance staff he'd hired. Painters painted the old plain fences a nice clean shade of white. The parking lot was paved over, and Chloe thought the country feel of a grass parking lot was lost.

And then all of a sudden, men in suits starting showing up. Sometimes they arrived alone, sometimes in groups, sometimes with stunning women who made Chloe's heart beat faster with an emotion she had to admit was jealousy. They arrived in long black limos, coming in to shake John's hand and cloister themselves in his office. They'd tour the grounds, then disappear for hours. Chloe figured he was making quite a dent in his whiskey collection, but no one knew for certain. He'd had his office door, actually the whole doorframe, too, replaced with one of heavy oak. And it had a working lock.

He hadn't been kidding when he said he loved wood. Either he wasn't chancing another break-in, or he wanted a wall of privacy between him and the townspeople.

There was a wall between John and Chloe, and it was stronger than wood. John had set up a post-office box in town for rodeo business, and now he went to pick the mail up himself. Mrs. Walters at the tiny post office said John's routine was the same every day: At lunch, he stopped in for the mail. Then he walked to Casey's to order a burger or a salad. He opened the mail while he ate his lunch. Then he put the mail in his briefcase and returned to the office, where he closed and locked the door, often only opening it for his suit-wearing visitors who arrived in the late afternoon.

Cody had tried to quiz the drivers of the limos, but they weren't about to discuss their well-heeled customers. It was all very mysterious.

It was clear that John had decided to do everything on his own, without her, without any of the local people's advice. The rodeo was now a total business operation. That's what they'd brought John in for, she thought sadly, a business barracuda who cared little about the small-town integrity of No Chance.

A week before the rodeo, a giant billboard was constructed near the main road into town. It read,

No Chance, Texas! Welcome to the smallest town in Texas with the state's best rodeo! Hotels, restaurants, and coming soon, a Ferris wheel guaranteed to view four counties— come ride with us!

A lot of grumbling met the billboard's pronouncement. Then, to everyone's shock, Cody announced that John was buying out Casey's and applying for a liquor license. More amazing, he'd bought up all the land surrounding the rodeo and was applying to change the zoning.

It seemed John intended to change the face of No Chance, turning it into a town of money-making ventures. Some folks said it was great that commerce would finally come to their corner of the world. Others agreed it would be helpful to have the extra tax revenue, to build schools and encourage people to move there.

No one complained until a rumor went around that the "hotel" John was planning would have a casino to rival anything in Oklahoma or Louisiana, in fact, something on the scale of Las Vegas.

The horse dung hit the fan.

"It's time to send City Boy back where he belongs," Mr. Pickle pronounced at a hastily called secret meeting. Mrs. Tucker, Mr. Hill, Mr. Pickle, Dr. Lambert and his wife, as well as Cody, Chloe and Erin were all invited to the clandestine powwow. Eyebrows were raised; men in seen-better-days jeans and worn western hats chewed tobacco and the occasional piece of gum ceaselessly.

"It's too late for that," Cody said, "we've invited the enemy right into our midst."

"*You* invited the enemy right into our midst, Cody," Mr. Hill said, his round face flushed. "You and your scheming! And you said no one would care more about our rodeo than family! Well, I guess you know better now!"

"Now, folks," Cody said, trying to calm the high ire in the room. They were hiding out in a back room of the Dancing Chicken, one of the few places John hadn't yet bought up—but only because Dr. Lambert's wife owned the restaurant, frying chicken herself and heaping mashed potatoes with gravy on Saturday nights. "Let's try to consider the good that's come out of City being here."

"John is very nice," Mrs. Tucker said, to a chorus of boos. "He pays his bills on time—"

"Yes, yes," Mr. Pickle said with a wave of his hand, "we all know Mr. Carruth's money flows freely through our town, like bad hooch in a bathtub. What we need to do is figure out how to get rid of him and his money."

Chloe felt sorry for John. He had no idea of the plotting going on behind his back. Sighing, she drank her soda and glanced at Erin, who shrugged. There was nothing any of them could do while everybody was so upset.

"I guess we could tell him," Cody said.

Dr. Lambert replied, "*You* could tell him, Cody. You brought him here."

"Yeah," Cody said, white tufts of hair standing up

around his wrinkled and concerned face, "but I've already warned him off of trying anything with Chloe."

"Dad!" Chloe protested, snapping to attention. "John wasn't trying anything with me at all!"

Everyone stared at Chloe. "He was the soul of chivalry around me," Chloe said, "and frankly, he seemed to have No Chance's best interests at heart."

"Come on, now," Mr. Hill said. He gazed around the room at his friends. His pipe glowed as he searched for words. "The man has no interest at heart except money."

"I fear that's true," kindly Mrs. Tucker said. "Still, before you boys go and run him out of town on a rail, shouldn't we voice our concerns to him?"

"I could go get him," Erin said. "John would probably appreciate being included in this meeting."

This brought somber gazes to Erin. Chloe sat up straighter next to her friend. "I agree with Erin. John should be here."

"I know he's home," Mrs. Tucker said. "He picked up the chocolate chip cookies I put out for him."

Mr. Pickle shrugged lean shoulders under his worn work shirt. "Go get 'im, then, if you think he dares to face any of us with his liquor licenses and casino talk."

There were rumblings at this. "I'll go," Chloe said quietly to Erin. "You try to keep them happy. Or at least mildly peaceful."

Erin nodded. Chloe slipped out the door, hurrying

to Mrs. Tucker's B and B. She found John's room number in Mrs. Tucker's register, then went to his door. Knocking briskly, she hoped she wasn't interrupting him with one of the female visitors who seemed to flow in and out of town in the black limos with the strange men so frequently now.

"Well, well," John said, when he opened the door. "If it isn't the town lawyer come to pay a call."

He wore Burberry boxers and nothing else. She'd never seen such a broad chest, such lean muscle rippling down strong legs. "John, I'd like to invite you to a meeting tonight," Chloe said. She was breathless, but that was because she'd rushed over here, not because of the man staring down at her, not connected at all to his state of undress.

He pulled her inside his room. "Did Mrs. Tucker see you?"

"No—"

"Good. Then we can have our meeting in here. You know," he said, pulling her into his arms, "I knew you'd eventually come around."

He kissed her, long and sweet and slow, and Chloe felt herself melting, even though she didn't want to. She remembered how well he kissed, and how thoroughly he kissed, and when he said, "Tell me more about this meeting," Chloe had to struggle to remember the purpose of her visit.

"Everybody's upset with you," she told him.

"Oh, I know." He leaned her back on the tufted white bedspread. "They're just running around trying to figure out how they let the fox inside the henhouse."

"Precisely," Chloe gasped as he began kissing her neck. "I'm so glad you understand their feelings."

"I didn't say that," he whispered against her neck. "I said I knew what they were thinking. You, I don't understand at all. For example," he said, nibbling at her lips, "why do you act like you're not attracted to me when I know you are?"

"That's silly," Chloe said, pushing at him and trying to sit up. "We're so completely opposite to each other that any type of relationship between us would be nothing more than sexual."

"Well, shame on us," John said. "We wouldn't want *that*." He kissed her, and she pushed against his chest—lightly, because part of her wanted to kiss and be kissed, and yet purposefully because she had guilty visions of the older people impatiently waiting for her return before they brought out the burning torches to find John themselves.

"John," she said, her whole body melting under his caresses, "they're waiting for us at the Dancing Chicken."

"The Dancing—let them wait," John said. "Right now, I'm busy entertaining a sexy guest."

"That's the problem," she said, jumping up from the bed. She noticed that Burberry slim-fit boxers didn't exactly hide everything an aroused male had, and it was more than past time for her to leave before she completely lost her good, country-girl common sense. "They want to talk to you about all these things you want to do."

"So I finally got to them," he said with a sigh,

standing to snatch up a pair of jeans he slid over those nicely muscled legs. When he jerked the jeans up over his hips, Chloe's throat went totally dry. *Rats. I want to experience what this hunky man is offering.* But then again, she didn't. All her life she'd been looking for love. Passion with nothing to back it up was just a cardboard excuse for wood. "What do you mean?"

He shrugged, pulled on a shirt. "Was it the casino or the liquor license?"

"You'll see soon enough." She turned her head, tried to collect her thoughts. "Anyway, I'll just meet you there." She needed to get out of the close quarters, needed to stop being tempted by too much gorgeous male. Her senses were starting to play tricks on her, teasing her with what she was missing out on.

John caught her hand as she was about to slip out. "Oh, no," he said, "now that you're here, you're stuck with me. You can be *my* bodyguard and legal counsel." And then he kissed her so sweetly that Chloe began to realize she had a problem. Despite her tough resolve, despite her father's loud and decisive wishes, she was falling for John Carruth.

"To hell with them," John said, "let them wait."

And the next thing Chloe knew, she was being tempted into bed by a billionaire who could own anything money could buy. She didn't care; she knew the risk she was taking in allowing him to test her heart. Chloe let John slowly undress her, and she undressed him, her heart in her throat. They kissed, hot, fast, then slow and sensual, taking their time.

When John took her into his bed, Chloe let herself

melt into his embrace. She savored every kiss, every nibble, every caress, rushing her hands over his back, his body, his buttocks.

When John finally claimed her, Chloe gasped, her whole body on fire, dizzily crazily craving the connection. He touched her heart, Chloe knew, and maybe, maybe he even took it for his very own.

But that was the danger, Chloe realized with a sinking heart, and what her father had been worried about. She'd fallen once for a magnetic male who talked smooth, and she'd learned the hard way just how easily she could be shattered.

Chapter Seven

"They'll come looking for us if we don't hurry," Chloe said, twenty minutes later. She pulled away from John as if he was getting too close to a wall marked No Trespassers, and John let her go. Reluctantly. Women didn't usually run from his bed, but Chloe would have to be different.

"They'll come looking for *you*. Not me." He'd rather stay here. She knew darn well he wanted her again. He knew she wanted him, too.

"You don't understand," Chloe said, handing him his jeans, still stiff and blue despite two washings. "We have to be careful to keep this…I mean…we don't want anyone to know. They'll never give us any peace."

She scrambled into her clothes, and John sighed. All this small-town, salt-of-the-earth stuff was cute, but it wasn't real life, and frankly, these people needed to get over it. "Let's pretend their opinions don't matter."

She opened the door and shot out like a rabbit.

John shook his head at her nervousness and her obvious guilt at what they'd just shared. "What does the Dancing Chicken serve?" he asked, following her.

"Fried chicken." Chloe glanced over her shoulder as she walked quickly down the sidewalk, practically running away from him, he thought. "And sometimes grilled, but not often. Depends on who's there to do the grilling."

He caught up to her, keeping pace with her long strides. "Well, that's all about to change. From now on, restaurants are going to be open standard operating hours, with dependable menus."

"John, you're going to invite a mutiny. Fair warning."

"I'm inviting change, which is exactly what's needed around here. A little discipline, a lot of direction."

"In your vision of the world, everything works smoothly. Everything is handed to you when you want it, and never are you inconvenienced. But the people in this town don't have personal valets, John. They don't have people to do their shopping and help to watch their children. When these townspeople, as you like to call them, have sick kids, they just don't open their restaurant that day. They don't like it, but life is what it is. They do the shopping for their homes and their restaurants themselves, they take their kids to the doctor themselves. They sit up at night with their children and their elderly family members, and by golly, sometimes they have personal emergencies as well that can't be helped." She stared at John, eyes bright with anger. "So you think about that sometime when you disparage whether the menus are 'dependable' or whether everything runs according to 'schedule.' We help each other in this town, we work hard, and we all love each other. And we don't need you laughing at us."

She gave him a last long look, then pointed to the Dancing Chicken. He could see several people standing on the patio, listening to Chloe, clearly agreeing with her opinion of him.

John shook his head and went up the wooden steps. He was in enemy territory; now it was time to smooth the pitching waters. He'd faced many an irate corporate board. This would be simple. "You folks want to speak to me?"

"Yes," Cody said, nodding as they all filed inside the Dancing Chicken and went into the back room. "All of us have voted," he said, not really giving John a chance to sit down, "and we want to buy you out, City."

John hadn't expected that. "How are you going to do that?"

"We don't exactly know," Dr. Lambert said, "but we know we wish we'd never brought you here, son. We're ready for you to hit the road with the next train, so to speak."

John blinked, glancing at Chloe. They'd really toss him out if they knew he'd just spent wildly satisfying stolen moments with one of the town's favorite daughters. "I'm sure that we can talk things over and reach a compromise everyone is happy with."

"No, we can't," skinny Mr. Pickle said. "You're not thinking about us. To you, our town is just an empty place begging to be filled up with whatever makes the most money. But that'll destroy our way of life. And we don't want it."

"We wanted you to fix the rodeo," Mr. Hill said, puffing on his pipe, "we didn't want you fixing everything. We liked what we had. Maybe we didn't know it until it was too late, but we know it now."

Mrs. Tucker nodded. "We like you, John, but perhaps you're too interested in what money can buy."

He shook his head. "You need investment here. There's nothing in No Chance. The plant has closed. The restaurants open when *you* want them to. You can't expect people to come to a rodeo when they can't expect even basic services. The nearest pharmacy is in Farmbluff."

"You sweat the small stuff too much," Mrs. Lambert said. "Not everybody lives with the convenience of everything being on the nearest corner. We don't need a coffee shop under every lamppost, you know."

"But those things bring jobs," John tried to explain patiently. "Surely you see that people here need jobs."

"We do." Mr. Hill nodded. "But we don't want those jobs to be trading in liquor and cigarettes and nekkid women."

"Naked women?" John's brows shot up. "I haven't seen a naked woman since I've been to No Chance."

For some reason everybody automatically glanced at Chloe. She blushed furiously and looked out the window.

"There'll be naked women when your liquor store opens," Mrs. Lambert said. "And when the liquor stores hit town, crime comes with them. And stores for marital toys. Prostitution. Graffiti on every wall. We just don't want it here."

"Well, I wouldn't mind seeing a naked woman occasionally," Mr. Hill said, and got booed roundly for trying to inject levity into what was clearly a deathly serious meeting. John looked around at the roomful of determined faces. A lot of what they were saying was true. He could understand their fears. What was normal for him was scary to them. "I'm sorry," he said slowly. "In my efforts to help the town grow, I have abused your faith in me."

They sat silently. He glanced at Chloe, who looked away again. "Mrs. Lambert," John said, "do you have some cold chicken, perhaps, and iced tea, that everyone could munch on? My treat, while we talk this over together."

"We don't want your bribes, son," Dr. Lambert spoke up.

Suddenly a voice said, "You don't have to eat his food if you don't want to, but at least give the man a chance to make matters right."

Erin jumped to her feet. "Jake!"

In all the heated discussion, no one had heard Jake come in. John studied his brother, wondering whose side he was on. He'd just bet that one of the kindly busybodies in this room had alerted Jake to the fact that John was about to get sent back to the city with a boot in his backside. He'd put his money on Erin. "Back to stay?"

Jake shook his head. "Farmbluff's fine for me."

If anybody would benefit by John returning to Manhattan, it would be Jake. He was uncomfortable with John's presence in No Chance. He stared at his long, lean brother and realization hit him. He hadn't even bothered to slow down enough to take in his relationship with his new brother, what it meant to be adopted, how he felt about having one person on the planet who was typed from the same DNA. Finding out he had a twin he'd never known about had freaked him so badly that he'd gone into overdrive doing the only thing he knew how to do. Make money.

No wonder he was unpopular as hell around here. *I'm like some freaking computer operating on a finance chip.*

"Chicken?" Mrs. Lambert asked, setting a platter of cold, tasty-looking chicken on the table. Erin went to the kitchen to bring out a large pitcher of tea, and Chloe fetched a platter of pretty glasses stamped with a label that read THE DANCING CHICKEN in bold white letters against the blue glass.

They were proud of their town. John glanced at Jake. His twin stood watching him, his own eyes looking back at him, and John knew that as much as he wanted to change these people, they'd changed him instead. "Chicken on the house, everyone," he said, never taking his gaze from Jake's until the moment that everyone jumped for Mrs. Lambert's good food.

Then he turned away to stare out at the empty main street of No Chance, his appetite gone.

"We can't avoid it forever," Jake said, coming to stand beside him.

"What?" John glanced at his twin while their friends dug into the food.

"The fact that we're splitting this town."

John blinked. "How so?"

Jake shrugged. "Folks don't know who to pull for. They're not sure if they want it your way or mine."

"What is your way? Running to Farmbluff?"

Jake shrugged. "The old way."

"And I'm the new way."

"Sure. Wouldn't you agree?"

"I suppose." There was a bigger question on John's mind. "Who told you about the meeting?"

"Chloe. Who else?"

John was astonished. He almost felt a tiny stab of betrayal. "I figured Erin."

"No. Chloe was afraid you'd get yourself in trouble here tonight."

"How so?" John demanded.

"She said by being pigheaded and stubborn." Jake shrugged. "That is a trait we share, so Chloe claims."

John shook his head. "So she was trying to save me from myself."

"She's in love with you," Jake said.

His brother's words washed over John. "I don't

think so," he said, even as he reveled in the hope. "And her father wants nothing to do with me."

"That's a problem," Jake agreed. "But Cody loves his daughter."

He sure did. Too much to let a city boy steal her away from him.

"You're going to have to make this right with the people," Jake told him. "And that's going to call for a compromise on your part."

"I see," John said. "You're supposed to be my conscience. Try to realize that the town doesn't share my vision. Their views are what's made the rodeo so unsuccessful. That is what you're getting at, isn't it? Do things their way, for the sake of peace? To win the woman?"

"Wow, they grow 'em cynical up north." Jake shook his head. "Why don't you ask the gang of grizzled heads what they want?"

"Because you know as well as I do that what they want is my money going down the drain right after theirs in an unprofitable chase after an unrealistic vision." He was feeling pretty bitter about that, actually. They really hadn't wanted his expertise, or his counsel of how to turn their rodeo around and bring tourist money to the town. What they'd really wanted was to exist in their time warp, mismanaging funds while they competed against a town, Farmbluff, that had better business skills. "I can't let that happen. I've come to care too much for No Chance."

"Listen up, everyone!" Jake called suddenly. "My brother has an announcement to make."

John stared at Jake, slightly annoyed. "I don't think I do."

"I think you do," Jake said, and John saw a steely glint in his brother's eyes. A dare.

"I know what you want," he murmured, "and I'm not going to have a face-off here right now, not tonight. This is not going to be a referendum on my plans for No Chance."

"Better now than later," Jake said. "You're running out of time to make friends here."

"I don't have to make friends to make money," John bit out, and Jake winked at him.

"It's a helluva lot easier if you do."

"All right," John said, beginning to think he didn't like his twin very much. And why should he? He was the white hat, the better man. *While I am just an interruption in their routine.*

"All right," he said under his breath to Jake. "Have it your way."

He dinged a teaspoon on a glass, cleared his throat. "Good townspeople of No Chance. The purpose of this meeting tonight is ostensibly to clear the air between us, right?"

Everyone nodded. Since they were all seated and eating happily, John figured they couldn't be stirred up enough to run him out of town. Full bellies usually meant contentment. "All right. I hear that there's some disagreement on how things should be run around here. Some of you are unhappy about the decisions you think I'm making, which you believe aren't particularly right for your town. I'm willing to listen."

They all smiled at him benevolently, liking this turn of events. "After all," John continued, "partnerships always make things run more smoothly. I apologize if my way of going about business here has seemed heavy-handed."

Murmurs of "It'll work out," and "You're a good man, John," were heard. John drew in a deep breath, smelling the good fried chicken, enjoying the camaraderie.

"But there's one thing I'd like from you in return," he said to his contented audience. "I'll agree to listen to you, if you'll agree to listen to me."

They nodded, their eyes bright. John looked suddenly at Cody, who was digging into Mrs. Lambert's chicken like there was no tomorrow. "Cody," John said, "you brought me here under false pretenses. You knew very well that finding out I had a brother would turn my life upside down. No one wants to learn that their family isn't exactly what they thought it was. And you did this all under the guise of offering me a business proposal."

"Well," Cody said, his chicken caught between his plate and his mouth before he could take another bite. "I was afraid if I told you outright that you wouldn't come here."

"Yes," John said, his voice low. "And yet, I did come. And even after I found out about your dishonesty, I've stayed."

"That's true," Cody said, "even though some folks said they wished you wouldn't. You do appear to be a stubborn cuss."

John smiled. "Well, then, you'll completely understand why I want to ask you right here, in front of the townspeople you consider your family—and whom I hope can be mine one day—if I may have your permission to pay court to your daughter."

The room went silent. Cody gulped, put his chicken down, wiped his fingers. He glanced around at all his friends, who sat waiting to see what his reply would be. John figured this was the only way he'd ever get wily Cody to give an honest reason for why he opposed John dating Chloe. His suspicion was that Cody simply didn't want to share his daughter. His biggest fear had to be that John might take Chloe off to Manhattan with him for good.

John glanced at Chloe, expecting to see her smiling at him. He was, after all, trying to be chivalrous to her and respectful of her father. Wasn't that what everyone in this town wanted from him? A sign that he was paying close attention to their ways?

To his surprise, Chloe tossed down her napkin and fled the diner. Everyone stared at him, their eyes huge. Cody had the grace to turn a bit red, matching his red bandana and checkered shirt.

"Smooth, bro," Jake murmured, laughter under his tone, but John was already heading out the door after Chloe.

Chapter Eight

John caught Chloe just as she made it to the barn. He figured she was heading for Brandy—her constant companion—and if he didn't head her off there, it would be hours before he saw her again. "Wait," he said, catching her wrist and turning her to face him. "Tell me what I did wrong."

Chloe stared up at John, her heart beating fast. "You surprised me, for one thing," she said, "and you embarrassed me. I resent that you didn't tell me that you were going to spring your request on my father. And in front of all our friends!"

"I had to ask for the right to court you in front of the extended family. If I'd asked Cody when he was alone, he would have said, 'Hell, no.' Basically that's what he said the other night, wasn't it?"

Chloe's lids lowered, hiding her thoughts, though she didn't remove her fingers from John's. He'd twined them between his bigger fingers, holding her against him without crushing her, without making her feel trapped. "I suppose so."

"And isn't every discussion of importance done in front of the extended family? Tonight, the gang was all there."

Chloe shook her head. "John, if I wanted you to 'pay court' to me, as you put it, I would prefer that you had asked me first."

"Chloe," he murmured, stealing a kiss, "you were never going to be tied down without a real strong rope. That's what this ice-maiden rumor is all about. You've let that be said about you so every man will keep his distance from you."

She gasped. "That's not true."

"And you use your father as a stonewall. If any male shows the slightest interest, Cody's there to shoo that suitor off, just like he would a pesky bull."

Chloe pulled her fingers away from John's hands and put them on her hips. "You've got me all figured out, don't you?"

"Don't I?"

Anger flashed through her. "I think you're trying to take the council's mind off your taking over the town and our rodeo with your very wrong-headed ideas."

"Explain."

"Oh, they're all buzzing back there now," she said, waving a hand toward the Dancing Chicken. "They're not talking about what an evil, money-grubbing businessman Cody foisted on the community. You can be sure they're slapping Dad on the back, asking him when they might get to plan a wedding."

"A wedding?" John's brows rose. "Isn't that jumping the gun a bit?"

Chloe smiled, realizing she'd found the perfect way to put a crimp in John's pursuit of her. She knew very well that he wasn't serious about her. Her father was right about John Carruth—he was a man who went after the challenge, no matter what it was, and the goal was simple.

Winning was all John Carruth wanted.

He would "win" her the second Cody gave his agreement that John could date her. But she could scare him away without Cody's help. "Yes," Chloe said, her heart breaking because she knew she was about to see the "real" John Carruth. "They'll never let you rest now. Every time you walk to the post office, someone will ask you when there might be big news. You'll think they're asking about the rodeo, but they'll really be asking about a wedding. That would be big around here, bigger even than the rodeo."

"Why?" John asked, looking a tad too innocent for her taste. "What's the big deal about a wedding? Why would they get so worked up about that?"

"Oh, it wouldn't be just any wedding," she said, "you're a lost member of this town. And the happy ending is that you've come home, fallen for a town girl, a daughter of a respected man of the community—"

"Cody? Respected?" John asked, his eyes twinkling. "Chloe, he's a clown."

Chloe stared at John. "I'm trying to show you the future, and you are not taking your own life seriously."

"Oh, I am. It's just one more lesson in small-town dynamics. I have to say I'm fascinated." He leaned down and gave her a smooch. "Anyway, finish your story."

She gave an involuntary, startled gasp. "Quit doing that!"

"Doing this?" John asked, taking her shoulders and kissing her until she couldn't remember the tale she'd been spinning to scare him off.

Chloe pulled away, putting one hand on his chest. "Stand right there, and let me finish my thought."

"All right." John smiled at her, slow and sexy. "But I hope you finish it soon. They're probably waiting back there for us to return. I'm sure they've got a watch posted at the window, and someone sitting on your father to keep him from challenging me to some kind of bull riding duel of chicken."

Chloe removed her hand from John's very broad, very fine chest. "You're the proverbial bad boy making good. You'd make our town famous, give us something to brag about."

He liked the sound of that. "I thought that was Jake. Isn't he the most daring bull rider?"

"But you're the lost son. And now they won't pass one day without wanting to see you and me at the altar."

"That's all I have to do to gain respectability around here? Marry a rodeo clown's daughter?"

She wanted to slap the smirk off of his handsome face. "You can laugh, but remember, you're in No Chance. I'm just telling you how it is."

He scooped her into his arms. "I like it when you tell me how it is."

"John! Put me down!" He was starting to make her nervous. She wasn't certain she trusted the gleam in his eyes.

"Where's the nearest dark place where I can have you to myself for about a week?"

That sounded lovely, breathtakingly tempting even, but Chloe wasn't about to fall for it. "John, if you really want to date me, march yourself into the Dancing Chicken and you let my extended family tell you what's wrong with everything you're doing to our town." She wriggled out of his arms—she was tall enough to give even a strong man like John more than he could handle, thanks to determination and a very fit body from barrel racing. Then she waited, watching the gleam in his eyes dim.

It was a challenge, the drawbridge this knight would have to cross over an alligator-infested moat if he really, truly wanted her. He couldn't use her as a buffer to fool the people about his true intentions.

"I don't owe them any explanation," John said, and Chloe nodded.

"That's true. I'm well aware of the legalese involved in your business dealings. And the truth is, you owe none of us much explanation, since you've bought up all the available land around the arena. You can build what you like, regardless of what we want. You can open casinos, liquor stores, whatever. Or you can ask us what we really want."

He stared at her silently.

"The only reason you hesitate is because I was never what you really wanted. You're using me as a smoke screen, a diversion to throw off the people of No Chance. And I have to tell you," she said softly, "I don't admire you for it."

And then she walked away, her heart completely broken.

JOHN STARED after Chloe, not about to chase her down again. God, she was a pistol. Spicy, saucy, complicated. He was crazy about her, and she knew it. And she planned to make certain she held him for ransom, not about to give him even a sliver of her heart until he changed all the plans for the town to suit her and what she called her "extended family."

He heard applause and turned around.

Jake grinned at him. "I got here in time for the grand finale."

"Do you always eavesdrop?" John was itching to take his bad temper out on someone. His twin was as good as anyone.

"When it suits me," Jake said. He perched on a wood rail. "Most times it doesn't, though. Truthfully, I just came to check on you, make certain our girl hadn't cut you to ribbons."

John rubbed his jaw. "For a brother, you're not much help."

"But did we want to be that to each other?" Jake demanded. "We're a little old to be glad to find out we have a duplicate of ourselves walking around."

John glanced in the direction Chloe had gone. He

thought he heard a horse's hoofbeats. She'd probably saddled Brandy and was off. He likely wouldn't see her again for days. "If you're my duplicate, I hope you're going through the hell that I am."

Jake laughed. "I'm not. You city folk have thin skins."

"I've never understood that," John said, sitting across from his brother, eyeing him the same way he would a stranger. "My skin is not thin. At least I stayed here instead of running off."

"I just thought I'd let you have the town, since you were hired to save it. The lone gun brought in to do it all."

John shook his head. "I wasn't ever going to succeed, was I? I wasn't really supposed to. Cody wanted us to know about each other, I was supposed to throw my money at the rodeo, try to put a hole in Farmbluff's plans. And then I'd realize what a losing operation a rodeo is for a greenhorn to operate, and I'd slink off with my tail between my legs. Poorer, but having given No Chance their latest reason to stay just the way they are."

Jake laughed. "Boring."

"Then tell me what it is."

Jake shrugged, stood, brushed off his hat. "Nah. You go back there and ask them what they want. I'm not going to do your dirty work for you." He grinned, put his hat on and brushed one finger along the rim in salute. "In the meantime, best of luck. I'm heading back to Farmbluff tonight. I've got a lot to do in the next few weeks."

John stood, feeling as if there was more to say to his brother. "Thanks for checking on me."

Jake nodded. "You'll do the right thing."

And then he disappeared into the dark night.

John shook his head, torn. Did he go after Chloe? Or go to his office and lock the door?

Jake's words rang in his brain. *You'll do the right thing.*

How the hell could a man know what was the right thing to do? These people had hired him to make their venture profitable, yet they were hopelessly stuck in the past. Like babies, they hadn't yet learned to walk in the world of finance. No Chance could be so much more than it was. It didn't have to be stuck in the past as a closed-plant town. Why couldn't they believe in his vision? There was so much here that could bring this town to life, give these people lives to live that weren't so hard: a pharmacy, good schools, corporate taxes to build whatever infrastructure they desired.

But they didn't really want that, he realized sadly. He had been a victim of his own dreams. That little girl he'd seen on the pony in the parade so many years ago—how he wished he'd understood her innocent joy in just the simple pleasures, like home, family and a black-and-white horse to call her own.

Chapter Nine

John wanted a drink, but he realized he was going to have to give that up if he really wanted the townspeople to believe in him. The whole idea of liquor and casinos and the like upset them, so if he truly wanted to understand them, he had to learn to live their way—over iced tea. He threw open the door of the Dancing Chicken and strolled in. Erin, Cody, Mr. Pickle, Mr. Hill, Dr. and Mrs. Lambert, Mrs. Tucker—they all looked far too innocent for him to believe they hadn't been watching for him to reappear from the barn. "Could I have a glass of iced tea, Mrs. Lambert," John said, "and perhaps some of that tasty chicken?"

She brought him a huge helping, and a large glass of tea in a Dancing Chicken glass. "Glad you came back," she whispered as she put a napkin and utensils at his elbow.

"Thank you," he said, and then he heard the sound of hoofbeats. Everyone turned to look out the window, except Cody, who sat staring at John, his whole face a study of confusion. John took a bite of the chicken, keeping his face calm as he waited for the rider to enter. He wasn't about to give Cody the satisfaction of reading his emotions, which at the moment were going crazy. He was more nervous than he'd ever been, and when Chloe strode in, he thought his heart would jump from his chest.

She seated herself next to John and said, "I'll have what he's having, please, Mrs. Lambert."

The room was so still a pin dropping would have sounded like a firecracker.

"Chloe," Cody said, and Chloe waved her hand at her father. "Dad, join us. John has something to tell everyone."

John raised a brow, but he kept on eating. He knew that Chloe was daring him, and frankly, he had a surprise for her. Everyone grabbed the nearest chair they could, leaning in so they wouldn't miss a word.

John took his time cleaning his fingers on the cloth napkin. He drank some tea, rolled his eyes with pleasure. "Delightful, Mrs. Lambert. We should franchise this chicken of yours."

"Oh," Mrs. Lambert said, blushing.

"I'm serious," he said, nodding. "It'd put the Colonel to shame."

Mrs. Lambert shook her head modestly.

"See, you folks think I'm all about making money, so you don't really trust me. You see me as a salesman, out to hoodwink you into becoming some kind of sinful paradise for money-spenders."

Mr. Hill puffed on his pipe. "Son, we don't really know what to make of you. You're nothing like your brother, that's for sure."

"And we're not sure you've got the Wheaties to stick it out with us," Mr. Pickle added. "You're used to things in life that start with a *W*."

John raised a brow.

Chloe whispered, "Wine, women, and wishful thinking."

"Thank you," he said, wondering why she'd come back. Why she'd sat down with him. Why she was seemingly trying to help him. Was it possible she'd decided she was giving him a chance to win them all over?

It was suddenly wildly important that he win Chloe. Everything else in his life would work out, if he won Chloe. John knew that as surely as he knew how to make money. He was in love with Chloe Winters, had been from the moment he'd laid eyes on her. She was his own little girl on the pony, grown into a beautiful woman who would challenge him and change him for the better.

"I give you back your town," John said, looking at each face as he spoke. "I'll sell you back your land. I'll even leave my investment in the rodeo as is. Or I can keep what I've bought. As far as the town of No Chance goes, however, it's yours. I went overboard with my vision. I fell in love with making money years ago. But now," he said, looking at Chloe, "I'd rather fall in love with something else."

Cody said, "Now just wait a minute…"

"Dad. Hear him out."

"I don't want to," Cody said stubbornly. "He's trying to weasel my daughter away from me because I wasn't up-front about what I was really trying to do when I sent the proposal to him. That's what these big businessmen do. There's always a price to pay, believe me. Don't let him turn your head, Chloe."

"It's all right, Dad," she said, giving her father a hug, her gaze steady on John, "You can't protect me from everything in life."

"I should never have brought you here," Cody said to John, but John shook his head.

"I wondered that myself. But now I know that this is where I belong." John smiled at the people he wanted for his own "extended family." "Where else would I find so many wonderful people to teach me how to really live life?"

They gave him benevolent smiles.

"But what about Farmbluff? What about our rodeo?" Dr. Lambert asked.

"I don't know what to tell you about that," John said, taking Chloe by the hand and helping her to her feet. "As far as this businessman's concerned, you'd best get your number-one cowboy back. Right, Erin?"

He hadn't forgotten about the redhead who was sitting very quietly in a corner, watching everything with serious consideration. She shook her head at him. "Jake is his own man."

"Still, my suggestion is—and it's only a sugges-tion—this town figures out how to get their cowboy back before the rodeo opens. As a man I very much admire once told me, 'You'll do the right thing.' "

And then he dragged Chloe out into the starry night with him. "So," he said, holding hands with her as though they were nothing more than schoolkids in the first crush of love, "what made you come back?"

"Wanting to see you do the right thing." Chloe stopped, stood on tiptoe, and kissed him. "I knew you would," she said softly, "something just told me that Jake's brother had to have some of those same amazing genes."

"Yeah, well," John said, drawing Chloe up against him, "you just concentrate on me."

"I'm going to," she said, pulling his head down to hers, "I'm going to teach you how to make love properly, and how to kiss all night long under skies where the stars still shine bright, far away from city lights. I'm going to teach you how to ride, and how to survive in a small town where everyone loves to run your business. You're going to be the happiest man alive," she promised, and John laughed.

"You've promised everything but the pony," he said, and Chloe smiled at him as he undid Brandy's bridle from the post outside and walked toward the arena.

He was a billionaire, he could buy his own horse if he wanted. She had plenty of horses he could ride, but she wanted to give him his dream. "Want to come back to my house?" Chloe asked. "I hear you're an insomniac and I think I've got just the thing to help you with that."

John grinned. "Only if you agree to marry me," he said. "I do have my standards. I can't spend the night with the woman I'm madly in love with unless I know she's going to be mine forever. I need a commitment. It's a sign-on-the-bottom-line thing I have." He kissed her deeply to make his feelings totally clear. He didn't mind compromising in this town on a lot of things, but he planned on making this lady his.

Chloe smiled. "Yes," she said, "I'd love to marry you, John Carruth. And I promise you'll hold my heart long after those new jeans of yours no longer have any blue left in them."

Hearing her say yes was even better than he'd thought it would be. It was as if he'd waited all his life to hear "yes" to the thing he'd wanted most of all. John looked into Chloe's shining eyes, and he knew that of all the things in the world his money had bought him, nothing would ever be as precious as the woman he held in his arms under starry night skies in No Chance, Texas.

THE BULL RIDER

Chapter One

Jake Fitzgerald picked himself up off the ground, cursed, jumped away from the bull determined to gore him. Two adversarial rodeo clowns from rival Texas towns, Cody from No Chance and his brother, Clem the Bad of Farmbluff, burst into sudden action, waving their hats and running around to force the snorting bull from the ring.

Apparently Cody and Clem the Bad had put aside their differences for the moment to pull a fast one on Jake and his twin brother John Carruth. Cody Winters had asked for Jake's good word on their behalf to John, new general owner of the No Chance rodeo, to allow them to work the event in the ring. Jake had assumed they meant to work as rodeo clowns, the act in-between riders to keep the audience amused, and Jake had told John that Cody could come to little harm by making people laugh. It was a job Cody had done before since he was too old to be a bullfighter, and Jake understood Cody's desire to participate in No Chance's big debut of the revamped rodeo.

But somehow Cody and Clem had convinced John, a city boy from Manhattan, that they were fit to be bullfighters, protecting the cowboys in the ring. New to everything about rodeo, John wouldn't have known the difference between a bullfighter and a rodeo clown, and Jake could easily see how his brother had been taken in by these two astute legends of shyster antics.

Jake took a deep breath, cataloged his body parts and saw that he was fine, probably no thanks to the wily Winters brothers. He should have expected the uneasy duo of Cody and Clem to do the unexpected. The thought sat uneasily on him that this time, somebody— one of the riders or Cody or Clem themselves—could get seriously hurt. *And it would be all my fault.*

Jake listened for his score amidst the applause— he'd made it to the buzzer—but suddenly Clem took a swing at Cody, who ducked and returned fire. The brothers rolled across the sawdust, locked in battle. An unwanted moment of sympathy hit Jake. He and his twin brother, John Carruth, had never really made peace with each other, not since they'd learned of each other's existence more than a month ago. He was still reeling, and Jake knew John was, too. They had an uneasy alliance because of the No Chance rodeo, but the relationship was still raw, tight with tension. The announcer hadn't called his score; everyone was too stunned by the two rodeo clowns duking it out. Scattered applause broke out as some of the audience thought Cody and Clem were putting on a funnyman's show.

It was no show, and someone's butt would be on the line for this unprofessional display.

Mine, damn it.

John wouldn't be happy about the fisticuffs. He'd sunk a lot of money into the rodeo trying to save it. At the moment Jake wasn't happy, because clowns weren't supposed to fight anything except bulls. Clem and Cody had gotten this job because it was considered a "small" rodeo. There were a lot of younger, hungrier bullfighters in much better shape, with better acts than Cody and Clem the Bad.

"Damn it, lay off!" Jake exclaimed, getting between the two men as they threw punches that impressed even Jake, who had a reputation as something of a tough guy. A fist whizzed past his chin, barely missing him, and Jake tried not to shove Clem the Bad to the ground, since Farmbluff, Texas, was his new sponsor, after all. Still, he'd known Cody for all the years he'd lived in No Chance—he couldn't toss *him* to the ground. He was stuck babying two grown men. "Stop," he growled, tempted to throttle both of them. "You're making asses of yourselves."

A few cowboys rushed in to help him separate the two. Cody sent one last punch past his brother's head but it didn't connect. Clem spat on the ground, blood dripping from his chin. "Our rodeo will whip yours in two weeks," he told Cody, "and you'll be out of business, you slow clown."

There was probably nothing worse than being called slow, especially by a brother. Cody and Clem couldn't even live in the same town; they stayed separate by thirty miles of country road. It was ironic that Jake found himself worrying about his brother's investment, too, particularly since Cody and Clem were an annoying reminder of Jake and John's stormy relationship.

John was a billionaire. Jake was a bull rider. So far, they didn't really see much of anything the same way. Cody and Clem glared at each other once more, then went immediately back to their duties, awaiting the next rider. If nothing else, they were professional once a rider was in the chute.

Jake grimaced, went to the exit now that the epic battle of the clowns was over. "Does anybody know what my score was?" he asked, heading over to a circle of cowboys.

"Eighty-five," someone yelled. Jake shook his head and went to change. Eighty-five wouldn't be good enough. He'd need a helluva ride the next round.

"Jake!"

He turned. Petite, flame-haired Erin O'Donovan made a beeline for him, which wasn't good luck. Jake preferred Erin to see him winning, and at the moment, he was not winning. It was best if he kept his mind on his riding and off Erin, a feat that bested him more often than bulls.

Still, he waited for her to catch up to him. Hadn't he always waited on Erin?

"Nice ride," she said breathlessly.

She was going to make him think about her, damn it, when he shouldn't be. He never laid eyes on those bow-shaped lips without thinking about smothering them with his. She never got near him that he didn't find himself leaning forward to sniff her gentle clean scent of some dewy flower. Like Clem and Cody, these days he and Erin lived thirty miles apart—like magnets, every time they got near each other, they burst apart. Still, he cared deeply for her. "What's on your mind?" He kept his tone curt, impersonal, just the freaking opposite of what he really felt about the good doctor Erin, which was tender and very personal.

"You know how I moved back to No Chance?"

A few weeks ago, about the time he'd signed on with Farmbluff, she'd left Farmbluff and returned to No Chance, ostensibly to be among her friends. He suspected she was avoiding living where they would see each other often. "Yes."

She gazed at him, her big eyes a winter's blue. "I was wondering if you'd allow me to rent your house from you," she said, her tone rushed as she recited unnecessary talking points. "I need to find a home to buy, but I'm also reestablishing my clinic. I'd like to focus on the clinic first and then on house-hunting."

He listened patiently, knowing all the while he would say yes to whatever Erin wanted. There was only one problem he could foresee with her request: Erin O'Donovan sleeping in his big, wood-framed, rough-hewn bed—all alone. "Sure. As long as you need." He'd planned to rent out the farmhouse anyway.

"Thanks," Erin said, her smile showing her relief. "If you tell me how much and on what day of the month you'd like me to send money for—"

He leaned over and kissed her—on the cheek, not on the mouth, where he was dying to kiss her for hours upon long, mind-blowing hours. He kissed her on the cheek, like the good friend she'd always known him to be. "Donate the money to the clinic," he said. "What's good for No Chance is good for all of us."

He headed off, away from her spell, determined to get his mind back on his game.

It would be nearly impossible. Just a fraction of an inch, and he would have had her lips under his.

He could almost taste them.

ERIN STARED AFTER Jake Fitzgerald, her new landlord and secretly the champion of her heart. She would never have asked him if she could rent his ranch house if she hadn't known that she was safe as robins' eggs in a nest there. Jake saw her as nothing more than a sister; she was hardly daring controversy into her life by using his house.

Anything romantic between them would only be wishful thinking on her part. The thought had never crossed his mind; he hadn't even blinked when she'd asked him.

She hadn't been honest about why she wanted to use his house, though. While she did need to focus on setting up her clinic, she had a greater purpose. The town of No Chance, Texas—specifically Cody the Clown and John Carruth, Jake's surprise twin brother and the billionaire investor of the No Chance rodeo—had asked her to try to sway Jake into riding again for his hometown, the second his contract with Farmbluff was up.

Money would not sway Jake. The townspeople involved in the subterfuge agreed on that. Jake cared as little about money as his brother John appreciated it.

Family would not convince him. Simply put, once Jake had found out that his family included a new, secret branch so unlike himself as to be cut from a different tree, Jake had moved to Farmbluff. John and Jake, twin brothers, strangers to each other, were destined to stay that way as far as Jake was concerned.

Cody, an expert on sour family relations due to his own relationship with his brother, Clem, had suggested Erin conjure up an appropriate lure to bring Jake back. No Chance wanted its star rider on the home team, but mostly, they just wanted Jake back where he belonged. It felt as though a part of the family had gone renegade on them, and no one, from Ida Lambert, owner of the Dancing Chicken diner, to Sheriff Rory Whitmore, felt Jake should have left.

Erin had moved to Farmbluff to keep distance between herself and Jake. Her crush on him was useless. She'd always loved him. He'd always treated her like a childhood playmate, one he perhaps enjoyed more than others, but nothing like the woman Erin dreamed of Jake falling in love with.

So, as the hour had turned late in the Dancing Chicken and all members of the small town's committee were exhausted with thinking of anything which might change Jake's mind, it was suggested that only she was the proper person to convince Jake. Erin had shaken her head. Said no. Protested.

In the end, she'd reluctantly said she'd give it a try. And it was Chloe Winters, John Carruth's fiancée, who had suggested Erin begin her campaign for Jake Fitzgerald from within his own house. Where better to corner one's prey than in their own lair?

Erin pointed out that the plan was somewhat overdone. There was no need to sneak up on Jake. Someone he respected just needed to ask him to come back, tell him that he had too much of No Chance's blood to switch allegiance to Farmbluff forever. In due time, when Jake was over the shock of having a new brother, a successful brother, a man who was as opposite to him as the sun was to the moon, Jake would be open to returning.

But privately even she didn't believe that, and if the plan of moving into Jake's house so she and Jake would have a reason for frequent contact seemed contrived, she didn't have a better suggestion. He was hardheaded, strong, silent. They might not hear from him for months—only able to keep tabs on him through the random scores posted on rodeo Web sites as he traveled around the United States. Sometimes his house was empty for a month or more at a time, with Cody or Sheriff Whitmore going by to check on it. Since she needed a place to stay anyway, Erin had reluctantly agreed to set out to try to catch a cowboy. She was doing it for the rodeo, of course; she was doing it for the hometown she loved.

It had nothing to do with her own secret hope of catching a bull rider of her very own.

"Doctor!"

Erin turned. "Yes?"

A cowboy she didn't recognize ran up to her. "Can you come check on Cody?"

She hurried after him. "What's wrong?"

"Oh, he and Clem were fighting, nothing much, just a bit of a squabble. You know how they carry on."

She didn't know this cowboy, hadn't seen him before this rodeo. He seemed very familiar with Clem's and Cody's feud, which had lasted for years. "Where are we going?" she asked as they jogged through little-traveled entrails of the back offices, heading toward the barns through a circuitous route.

She never got an answer. Someone grabbed her, slapping a hand over her mouth, and Erin was shoved onto the floor of a dark stall. Tape was clapped over her mouth, her hands and ankles bound, a burlap sack dropped over her head so fast that she couldn't see who was in the stall with her. They worked silently, and then the stall door closed. Erin sat stunned in the hot, dirty stall, shocked and scared.

When I find out who's behind this prank, I am so going to kick their butts!

Chapter Two

It seemed an eternity passed before someone opened the stall door.

"What the hell?"

The sack flew off her head, and Jake's handsome face was suddenly there. "Erin! What the hell happened?"

Gently, he pulled the tape from her mouth. Erin had never been so glad to see anyone in her life. "I'm fine," she said, "just get me out of here."

He quickly undid the binding on her ankles, rubbing them. "Who did this?"

"I don't know. I'm going to give them a piece of my mind when I figure it out."

He undid her hands, checking her wrists, then moving warm, reassuring fingers over the cramped bones. "I'll personally whip whoever did this to you."

"I'll let you. Right now, I just want out of here. I have to go check on the riders. No one has gotten hurt, have they? I'm pretty sure I've been in here about three hours." She checked her watch. "Actually, only about an hour and a half, thank God."

"You're not going anywhere," Jake said, helping her to her feet. "Erin, whoever did this is somewhere at the rodeo. You just can't walk around like everything is normal."

"I'm the doctor on call for these cowboys," Erin said, her tone now professional and deliberate. "No one is going to keep me from helping them."

"You haven't been doing your job for an hour and a half," Jake said, not expecting any other response from his childhood friend. Erin had too much habañero pepper in her to let someone scare her off. "I'm overruling you on this one."

"You're not," Erin said. "Jake, don't push me right now. I've been manhandled and tossed in a dirty stall. I'm going to do whatever it is someone doesn't want me doing."

He admired her spirit. He always had. "Nope," he said, "it's not about your job, Erin. Think. Why would someone want to kidnap you?"

"Kidnap me?" She stared at him. "Hiding me in a stall doesn't constitute kidnapping. Where is Sheriff Whitmore, anyway? He needs to know what happened in case anybody else goes missing."

Jake caught Erin's delicate chin between his fingers, forcing her to stare into his eyes. "Calm down," he said. "You're running a mile a minute." He gazed down into her eyes. "Don't be scared."

"I am *not* scared," she protested, and he itched to kiss her sweet lips.

"You've had a shock, and you're going to let me take you away from here until you've had a chance to work out your emotions. Cry it out, whatever."

She jerked her chin away from his hold. "What I need right now is action, not sympathy. If I was a man, would you suggest I need to cry it out?" she demanded, indignant.

He grinned. "I'd tell you to tough it out and go kick some ass."

"I'm going to go do my job, and you're not stopping me."

He swept her up into his arms. "Yeah, I am. Now you be nice and quiet and don't cause a ruckus while I sneak you out of here. You're not thinking clearly right now, but I'll think for both of us."

She gasped, flailed in his arms but not enough to dislodge herself, he noted. "Just let me take care of you," he said. "I promise you'll like it."

Erin stopped struggling in his arms, which was good because then Jake could walk to his truck faster. His main goal was that no one see him leave with Erin. Someone wanted her out of the picture, and he needed time to process the "whom."

"When did you turn into such an overbearing jackass?" Erin asked sweetly.

Jake set her down, unlocked his truck. He gave her a slight shove so she'd get the hint to get inside. "When I saw you tied like a turkey at Christmas. Now, fasten your seat belt."

FIFTEEN MINUTES LATER, Erin wondered if she was having a delayed reaction of rage. Certainly, she wanted to be mad at Jake and his whole ride-off-with-my-lady routine, but she was beginning to suspect he was right. She'd listened as he called Sheriff Whitmore on his cell phone, telling him what had happened, instructing him where to find the stall and the ties that had bound Erin. Hearing Jake recite the details of her story ratcheted up some latent stress she'd refused to acknowledge. He and Sheriff Whitmore had discussed getting another physician on call for the cowboys, which Erin hadn't appreciated in the least. How dare Jake take over her job? Especially a role that was so dear to her heart?

She saw that her hands were trembling and as a doctor, began to accept that perhaps she needed to allow him to do for her what she was unable to do herself—think clearly.

"I'm sorry," she said when he'd parked his truck and led her inside his house. "I'm being a cow."

"Yes," he said, pushing her down onto the leather sofa. "But I expect and admire that in you. I'm going to make you a cup of tea right now, and I expect you not to move off that sofa. Feel free to put your feet up."

She had too much adrenaline running through her to be treated like a swooning heroine in a novel. "Jake, don't take the hero stuff too far."

He laughed. "Ah, my old Erin returns."

"Yes. I'll make the tea." She glanced around the kitchen, sighing with comfort. "I love this house."

"Good thing you'll be renting it from me, then," he said. "See? Everything works out for the greater good." He took the kettle from her, setting it on the stove. "Now that you've calmed down, let's talk about whose bad side you got on."

"How do you know I did? How do you know that some random weirdo isn't running around No Chance's rodeo?"

"Because we already have the cast of weirdos in town right now. The first person who comes to mind who might do this is Clem the Bad."

"He was working the rodeo. In fact, he and Cody got in a fight."

Jake nodded. "I know. Did you hear any voices?"

She tried to think. "It all happened so fast—"

"That's okay. Something may come to you later."

His voice was soothing, calming. Erin shook her head, unable to make herself think deeply about what had happened. "Are you thinking it was an attempt to make No Chance's rodeo look unsafe?"

"We have to consider that."

Erin sank back into the leather sofa, let Jake bring the teacups out. "Maybe there's something to this fainting-heroine thing," she said, suddenly feeling weak.

He put a warm afghan over her feet, smiled the sexy smile at her that she'd always loved. There was no place she'd feel safer than Jake's arms.

"I'm going to go make a couple of phone calls," Jake said. "Do you want to watch TV? Oprah, maybe?" he asked with a wink. "Dr. Phil?"

Erin tossed a pillow at his back as he left the room.

Jake's laughter made her smile, and suddenly, the trembling subsided.

ERIN WASN'T CERTAIN when she fell asleep, but she slept like a bear in winter. When she awakened, it was nine o'clock at night. The moon shone in the window of Jake's house; he'd left a small light burning near the television. A note lay on the coffee table beside her. Reaching over, she picked it up.

Gone for my second ride. Stay here, stay safe. I'll be back soon. Shotgun is loaded and in the office. Call my cell if you get scared, but don't tell anyone at all—not even Chloe—that you're here.

The trembling started up again. "Darn it," she said, getting up to make certain the front door was locked. It was. She knew Jake wouldn't have left her in an unlocked house, but her nervousness had returned. She didn't want to think about why she needed to know where his shotgun was. She wanted to go watch him ride. All her life, one of her favorite things to do had been watching Jake at the rodeo. Okay, it was nerve-racking—she worried like crazy about him. When he got hurt, part of her heart hurt. When he rode well, she experienced his pride and happiness. She would never tell anyone that she felt this way, but loving Jake was so easy that she'd never given her feelings a second thought. "I hate being a prisoner," she muttered, drawing the drapes. If she called someone to find out what the scores were, they'd ask why she wasn't at the rodeo.

She didn't dare go against Jake's wishes. Of the two of them, he was thinking more clearly. Wasn't he?

Biting her lip, she stared at his phone, recalling that her purse was locked in the trunk of her car at the rodeo. She didn't carry anything on the grounds with her when she was working except her medical bag. She hadn't had a chance to get that out of the trunk before her shift, either. She'd gone in to watch Jake ride, and then…

She shook her head. And then suddenly, she did remember—black boots with silver tips.

Just as the sack had been thrown over her head, her head had been pushed down. She'd seen the boots, the owner's feet bracing as he'd worked to tie her.

No. There had been two people, at least. Someone had covered her eyes while someone bound her mouth.

A knock on the front door sent a tight scream from her throat. She ran into Jake's office to hide, to be near the safety of the shotgun. It was on the wall in its hooks but she felt only slightly comforted by it. Louder, more impatient knocking ensued for a moment, and then she heard the doorknob jiggling. She locked the office door with nervous fingers, grabbed the shotgun off the wall, waited, her breath held.

"Erin? Erin, it's John."

"Oh, dear God!" Erin muttered, putting the gun

back on the wall. Jake's fraternal twin brother, not a bogeyman. Jake's over-cautious warning had her spooked.

She forced herself to walk like a normal human being—not run like a frightened rabbit—to the door. "What are you doing here?"

John Carruth smiled at her. "Jake sent me to keep you company."

Jake and John weren't the best of friends—not yet—but perhaps the relationship was slowly coming around. After not knowing about each other for thirty-two years, the brothers had developed a secret partnership to save No Chance's rodeo. Even though Jake was riding for Farmbluff—the enemy town—Erin knew he still wanted the town of No Chance, and its rodeo, to succeed. "Thanks for coming," she told John.

"No problem. Anything I can do for you?"

"Tell me the scores."

He laughed. "Jake got a 91."

"That's better than he rode before! Was he happy?"

"No. You're here. You've got him worried. Someone tried to kidnap you, he said. What the hell is going on, Erin?"

John was from Manhattan, had made a lot of money being a big cheese in a sophisticated world. Small-town life was new for him, but he loved No Chance and the town was really beginning to embrace him. He had asked Erin's best friend, Chloe Winters, to marry him, and they were planning the event for August. Cody the Clown was Chloe's father, and he couldn't stop bragging about his new son-in-law-to-be. Erin sat on the sofa, motioning John to join her. "I don't really know what happened. I'm only now beginning to remember bits and pieces—"

Erin's heart nearly stopped when John eased back into the leather sofa and crossed one leg over the other, his handsome face smiling as he listened.

He was wearing black, silver-tipped boots.

Chapter Three

"What is it?" John asked. "You look like you've seen a ghost."

Erin shook her head, her mind racing. John would never hurt her—she knew that. It was only a strange coincidence that he wore the same boots as the man who'd shoved the sack over her head. Jake trusted John. She took a deep breath. "Talking about what happened is unpleasant, I guess," she said, thinking first. "I just need to keep my mind on something else."

"I understand," John said, and Erin knew he did.

"New boots?" Erin asked.

John grinned, running a hand proudly over the boot's shaft. "There's a guy who makes these and sells them in one of the stalls we rented to vendors. Gave me a great deal on this pair." He looked so proud of his boots—and so guilt-free—that Erin wondered if her mind was playing tricks on her. But no, she remembered those boots clearly.

"They're selling like hotcakes," John said. "There must have been five other men lined up to get a pair."

"Just like those?"

He nodded. "Just the same. They came in a few other colors, but the black was by far the most popular. I believe Dr. Lambert even bought a pair."

They were handsome boots. Erin tried to swallow past the tightness in her throat. If so many pairs had been sold, it would be nearly impossible to identify her kidnapper solely on a description of boots. "I wish they'd been one-of-a-kind," she murmured, thinking out loud, and John nodded.

"Me, too. I commissioned him for a pair made-to-order. I plan on wearing them when Chloe and I get married. But don't tell her."

His face lit up at the mention of marriage and Chloe, and Erin had to laugh. Some of her unease ebbed away. "I won't."

"I bought Chloe a pair for a wedding present. Hers are about worn out."

"She would say they're just getting comfortable," Erin said.

"I know. But these were such pretty boots. They had a white shaft with pink roses on them."

Erin smiled. "She'll probably wear them in competitions."

"She'll probably wear them to our wedding," John said. "I'm prepared for that." He looked very pleased about marrying a woman who would wear boots to a wedding, and the last of Erin's doubts melted away.

"Funny thing about those boots," she said, "the guy who dragged me off was wearing a pair just like yours."

John stared at her. "Black with silver tips?"

She nodded, searching his face.

He stood. "Does Jake know?"

She shook her head.

"Sheriff Whitmore needs to be informed that you have a description."

"But you said the man was selling the boots like hotcakes," she pointed out. "And besides, I don't know that Jake has told the sheriff what happened."

John slowly sank onto the sofa. "I hope to hell he has. The rodeo doesn't need a criminal running around. What if this guy's figured out you're missing and tries to kidnap someone else? Let's call Jake and at least tell him about the boots." He dialed his brother on his cell phone.

"Hey, Jake. No, Erin's fine. I don't know where you're at in your investigation about what happened, but Erin says the guy was wearing black, silver-tipped boots."

John listened, then nodded. "I know. I bought a pair myself. Have you told the sheriff?"

They exchanged more information, then John disconnected the call. "He asked if you were all right. I told him you're fine."

"I am. I know you've got a lot to do with the rodeo, John. Don't feel like you have to babysit me."

"I don't. But I am going to leave now. Jake wants me to talk to the vendor, see if he'll let me look over his credit card receipts to try to figure out who else bought a pair of these boots." He looked at her, worry in his eyes. "Can I at least send Chloe over?"

"No, thank you." She shook her head. "Chloe

needs to think about her event. She wants to win in barrel racing tonight. I'll be fine by myself."

"You're safe here. Lock up tight and don't open the door for anyone. Jake says no one's got a key but me and him and Cody."

"I have Jake's key," she said softly.

"Good work," John said, referring to the initial plan that she figure out a way to lure Jake back to No Chance. "If anybody can talk him into giving up his crazy notion of living in Farmbluff, it's you."

"I'm not so sure about that." Yet she hoped it was true.

"He's stubborn," John said with a smile as he let himself out. "It runs in the family, apparently."

She closed and locked the door behind him, the nervous jitters returning now that she was alone. But she was safe, as John had pointed out. It could have been a random incident, too, which she hadn't previously considered, which would mean no one was looking for her. There was no reason for anyone to want to kidnap her. Erin let out a long breath, settled back onto the sofa.

The best thing she could do was sit tight. Everything was going to be all right.

Still, she couldn't relax. After a moment, she went down the hall to Jake's bedroom. Flipping on the light, she took in the lowered wooden blinds, the lamps, the bedside reading material, the wide, masculine bed covered in a spread with a Western motif. The room was comfortable, inviting. It somehow felt safe.

She'd never been in Jake's bedroom. Everywhere she looked, everything she touched, was a part of him. She'd never been this close to him, which was as much as he'd let her, or anyone else, be close to. Intimacy was not Jake's thing. He'd dated lots of women, Erin knew, but she didn't think anyone had ever touched his heart or claimed a meaningful part of his life.

There was a first time for everything. He'd offered his house, and she was lured by the chance to touch a part of him. Erin pulled off her boots and slipped under the covers.

ERIN AWOKE with a gasp, aware that someone was in the room with her.

"It's okay," Jake said, but Erin couldn't stop her heart racing. He flipped on the lamp and the room filled with light. Dressed in jeans, a black hat, a dark Western shirt, the bull rider struck a commanding pose. Erin knew her heart wasn't racing now because of fear—staring up at Jake from a bed had her mind going places it shouldn't. Maybe it was the steamy, dark-eyed look he wore that made her wonder if his thoughts weren't traveling in the same direction as hers.

"I didn't mean to scare you," Jake said. "You're a very sound sleeper. Not even a snore." He grinned.

She sat up, indignantly plumped a pillow behind her back. "I only snore when I drink wine. I don't know why, so don't ask."

He sat on the bed. "I don't snore at all."

"You could be chivalrous and say you do."

"I'll be chivalrous and offer you a cup of tea."

Her brow crooked. "Why would you offer me a cup of tea at this hour?" The bedside clock couldn't be right—or it really was two o'clock in the morning and Jake was more like his brother, insomniac, than he realized.

"I want to set the stage," he told her. "I want to be certain I have your full attention."

Her gaze wandered for a split second across his chest. Oh, he had her attention, but perhaps not the way he intended. "Go on," she said, "I'll skip the tea."

"We caught your attacker. Even as we speak, he's comfortably housed with Sheriff Whitmore."

She gasped. "Why didn't you just tell me?"

"I told you, I was setting the stage."

"Oh, because you're the hero in the play," she said, getting it.

"And because you're going to love knowing who it was, and how we caught him."

There was no reason to lie in this bed. Now she was too amped, and sex was definitely not a possibility—even if Jake had ever considered it, which she was pretty sure he hadn't. This was going to be a problem. She was thinking about it, and he wasn't. *Not good news, Dr. O'Donovan.*

Rats.

She was getting caught in her own trap. Maybe that had been Chloe's intention all along. "Go on," she said, padding down to the kitchen. "I'll put the kettle on, but don't take too long dramatizing your heroics. You do have one last ride tomorrow, don't you?"

"Yes." He pulled off his boots while she went into the kitchen. "I won't say it's a hardship coming home knowing that you're here."

Erin blinked, stared across the counter into the den at Jake. "Are you being nice or flirting or something in between?"

He shrugged. "I take one lump of sugar with my tea."

"Come in and fix it yourself." She pulled down two mugs, both black, that read Bull Riders Do It Better. "Have much of an image problem?"

He laughed. "No. Anyway," he said, coming into the kitchen and taking out the box of tea, "your clue about the boots was helpful. Sheriff Whitmore and I decided to lie in wait at the stall where I'd found you, see who returned for you. I'll give you three guesses who wanted you all to himself."

Erin didn't want to guess. It had been too frightening. She was still too angry. "If you don't tell me at once and quit torturing me, I'm going to use a spatula on you in a way you really won't like."

He grinned. "Clem the Bad."

"Not possible," she said slowly, "he was in the ring fighting with Cody."

"That's true. But apparently, he'd overheard you and me talking about you returning to No Chance, that you weren't going to be living in Farmbluff anymore. He also heard that you were going to rent my place. Their rodeo is in two weeks, and apparently, he and his cronies decided they couldn't take the chance that you might try to talk me into returning to No Chance for good."

"Why would they think that?"

"Because Cody had bragged to Clem that No Chance was going to hire me away from them. He said his daughter Chloe had come up with a great scheme, one that involved you enticing me to ride for No Chance."

Erin gulped. "I would really have to be a manipulative person to do all that."

He looked into her eyes, his blue ones searching her gaze. She could hardly hold still; her secret was bursting inside her.

"Well, it was an intriguing premise, but I can't see you doing anything underhanded anyway," Jake said. "It was a bit far-fetched for me, though good for my ego."

She looked at the Bull Riders Do It Better mug that he had filled with hot water for her. "We wouldn't want your ego to suffer."

"So the idea was to kidnap you, take you away somewhere far away until after the rodeo. I believe the plan was to take you to Mexico. Clem has a place there, and a señorita who keeps the place up for him."

"Good thing Clem's in jail, or I'd go give him a taste of his own medicine," Erin said. Whatever Clem had in Mexico wasn't as nice as the house Jake had. No doubt it was so far away from civilization she'd die of thirst or snakebite if she tried to walk back to the States. Without some type of American paperwork, she'd have a hard time getting back into the country unless she could find an understanding border guard. She swallowed, sipped some tea. "I just don't see how he thought I was such a problem. Don't you have a contract with Farmbluff?"

He nodded. "That's what I told Clem. But he said my heart wouldn't be in the riding if I knew you were back here." He gave her a long look. "It isn't true, is it? You didn't have a plan with Chloe and Cody?"

"Oh, no," Erin said, shaking her head, her eyes wide-open and innocent. "Well…yes," she finally said, unable to lie to him.

He turned off the gas and set the kettle to the side. "Tell me all about it."

She sighed. "Jake, No Chance doesn't want you riding for Farmbluff. Obviously, your brother wants you to be part of his world now, and help make his rodeo a success."

Jake gazed at her. "You're saying that John is involved in the scheme?"

"And everybody else in the town that you know and love," Erin said impatiently. "Did you really think you could leave, ride for the enemy side, and your family and friends wouldn't plot to get you back?"

"I didn't suspect they'd use *you*."

"Well…" Erin thought quickly, not wanting him to guess how she felt about him. "I was the likely candidate. I drew the shortest straw, for one thing."

"Oh, the straws again."

She nodded. "You know that's how we settle things in No Chance."

He looked disappointed. "I liked the idea of you being a trap so much better."

She blinked. "A trap?"

"Like a female spy with designs on the hero of a thriller." He walked into the den, put his tea on the coffee table. "Didn't hurt my ego at all."

"Sorry I couldn't help," Erin said, following his lead. "It could just as easily have been Mrs. Lambert who was picked to make No Chance's case. They really are hurt that you left, Jake." It was a small fib in the scheme of things, wasn't it? He didn't need to know her true heart's desire. Best to let him think her part had been purely by chance, a town ploy. "But let's just play 'what if' for a second," she said, dangerously curious. "What if I had intended to use my feminine wiles on you?"

"Oh," he said with a smile that made her bones tingle. "I intended to capture you and make you tell me all your secrets."

"Ha! I wouldn't."

"You would," he assured her. "I have some very convincing methods."

She'd just bet he did, honed to a fine art by various members of the grateful opposite sex. "Back to Clem," she said, tearing her mind away from all the wonderful visuals her mind was conjuring of naked her and naked Jake and endless delight. "What happens to him?"

"Well, he's been a very bad man, as usual." Jake pushed pillows behind him more comfortably, settled in. "I shouldn't have vouched for Clem to work at the rodeo, not that that matters right now, I guess. I thought he and Cody could use a chance to practice their comedy routine and get closer as brothers." He sighed. "Anyway, I knew what I was doing when I signed on with Farmbluff. I knew Clem worked for that paper-plant owner, knew he was just a dishonest guy who didn't mind being underhanded if it suited him, and by then knew that's where the money for my sponsorship was coming from. I had the idea that if I lived in Farmbluff, gained their trust, I could figure out how they planned to undo No Chance's rodeo. I was making some progress, I had a good contract with them, and frankly, once John came to No Chance, I needed some space. And you," he said, gently tugging on a lock of her long curly red hair, "had been living in Farmbluff. Moving there seemed like a no-brainer to me."

Her breath caught. "I don't see that where I live has anything to do with the story."

Jake looked at her, tugged at the flame-colored strand again. "Let's just say I've always had a thing for the color red."

Chapter Four

Erin stared at Jake for a split second, knew he was teasing her, felt her heart shift and then drop inside her. He was playing around, and yet something inside her—hope—had jumped to life, breathing joy that Jake would move because of her.

So smooth. She got to her feet, shook her head at him. "I'm not buying, cowboy. And here's the thing—I'll probably be out of your hair again tomorrow. Right now, I'm going back to bed." Going down the hall, she snagged one of the pillows from the king-size bed. She went back to Jake, tossed it to him. "You know where the blankets are."

He grinned at her. "They say it's good luck to 'get lucky' the night before a ride."

She raised a brow. "Gee, guess you'll be riding without that extra sprinkling of fairy dust. Goodnight, Jake. And thanks for getting me out of that stall. I never realized before how claustrophobic I am." She really was grateful; she shivered just remembering what might have happened if Jake hadn't come along. Still, she couldn't fall for his teasing.

"Not a problem. Turn the lights out when you go." He settled down on the sofa, and Erin turned the lights off. She stood there for a second longer, wondering if she was being unfair by taking his bed and making him sleep out here, and then the sound of contented snoring made her jaw drop. "Typical male," she muttered, and went to bed.

He hadn't even blinked an eyelash when she'd said she'd be out of his hair tomorrow. That's what she got for falling even an inch for his slick words about loving red.

JAKE WAITED until he heard the bedroom door close, then got to his feet. He hadn't been completely honest with Erin. He'd spun her a pretty good story, tried to put her mind on another track with some good-natured byplay, most of which he would mean wholeheartedly if he hadn't uncovered some disturbing information.

Erin hadn't been a target of Clem the Bad simply because of Jake. Erin had been on her way to a remote ranch in Mexico, Jake and Sheriff Whitmore had learned, but for a completely different reason. Clem's employer trafficked people across the border from Mexico into the States, people who camped at Clem's ranch until transportation could be arranged. A disease had broken out and several people had fallen ill. The local hospitals were too far away for them to travel to, and anyway, they were too ill to travel. Far cheaper and easier would be to bring a doctor to them. Erin would have had no idea where she was. It was the perfect plan, as far as they were concerned.

The only thing they hadn't counted on was Jake rattling Clem's cage until he had finally confessed. Clem and his partner in crime needed a couple of aspirins once Jake had finished with them. He'd barely been able to suppress the rage inside him. Lying in wait for the person who'd trussed Erin up, Jake had realized something—it had taken a year off his life to find her like that. Maybe it had been seeing her bound, or maybe it was the fact that she seemed so tiny and helpless, but his heart had practically stopped when he'd found her.

Clem he'd only slightly tapped on the jaw, just enough to give him a reality check of who he was dealing with. His partner, a little more reluctant to share his details of the story, hadn't fared as well.

And when it was all over, Sheriff Whitmore noted dryly, "Think you care an awful lot about that gal." Jake had just shrugged, but Rory's words were true.

Jake hadn't told Erin that he'd immediately broken his contract with Farmbluff. He hadn't told her he wasn't riding tomorrow. He'd broken small bones in his hand giving Clem and his buddy what they richly deserved, a fact he'd concealed from Erin. The rodeo doctor John had brought in to replace Erin had said he probably couldn't ride for at least a month—it was his rope hand—so Jake had withdrawn from his ride tomorrow. The No Chance rodeo was a success at least on a small scale for this year, so he didn't feel like he'd backed out on his commitment to John.

It was beginning to settle on him that he had a twin brother and that was something good in his life. When he needed someone to come check on Erin—Jake knew he'd be a mess if he was worrying about her being here alone—he'd automatically known John was the one person he could send. He trusted John, he realized, in a way he never thought he would. As he trusted no one else.

To his credit, even though he was probably crazy with rodeo responsibilities, John had immediately agreed to sit with Erin, make sure she was all right.

A tapping at his front door sent Jake to his feet. "What the hell?" he muttered. "Who the hell is it?"

"It's Cody!"

Jake opened the door. "At three-thirty in the morning?"

Chloe's father, the beloved rodeo clown, invited himself inside, his white hair wild, the paint on his face creased and smeared and somehow pathetic. "Clem told me what happened. Jake, you can't do this to my brother."

Jake frowned, closed the door. He pointed Cody to a chair. "I didn't do anything to Clem. He did it to himself."

"Look, put yourself in my shoes. If it was John, and he was in jail, wouldn't you want him out?"

Jake shrugged. "Not likely to happen." He didn't want to think about it. What would he be willing to do for John? Now he owed him. And John had offered him some kickback for rodeo entrants, whatever Jake could pull in. Their lives were beginning to become entwined.

It was an uncomfortable realization. They needed each other, and Jake wondered who needed whom the most.

"Listen, you roughed Clem up pretty good." Cody held up a hand. "And I'm not saying he didn't deserve it. I'm just saying, enough's enough, don't you think? He's too old to be in jail."

Jake's brow creased. "He wasn't too old to get into a rodeo ring with bulls. I still have a bone to pick with you about that. You told me the two of you were merely going to work on your act." He'd fallen for it. With John's recent appearance in his life, Jake had been an easy mark for a tale of brotherly bonding.

"Well, you know how it is," Cody said sheepishly. "These young guys don't know squat. We figured we could show the young guys the ropes, keep the riders safer. Nothing's more important."

"For the record, I'm aware you're not being honest." Jake tried not to think about his aching hand. He wanted sleep. Mostly he wanted Cody to disappear. "Can we discuss this in the morning? I'm just shy of beat."

"Tell Sheriff Whitmore to release Clem, Jake," Cody pleaded.

"I already vouched for you and your brother once, and you made me look stupid." Jake shook his head. "I wouldn't fall for that trick twice, Cody. Sorry."

"Clem has a bad ticker, just like I do. He'll never survive jail, a trial, anything like that."

Jake shook his head. "Then he shouldn't be involved in illegal human trafficking. Cody, we've got him in jail for kidnapping Erin. He's lucky he's not swinging for his bigger sins. Trust me, I'm probably saving him from himself."

Cody drew himself up. "You're lying."

Jake looked at his long-time friend. "About what?"

"Clem did not try to kidnap Erin. He wouldn't have done that."

"He said he did."

"He had no legal counsel," Cody shot back. "Remember, I put a child through law school, son. I learned a little bit while Chloe was studying all those years. Any dumbass knows you can't rough someone up and get them to say what you want them to. You and Sheriff Whitmore would be in big trouble if this ever got out." Cody stared at him. "I think you ought to appreciate the fact that I'm trying to help you, Jake."

So blood *was* thicker than water. Jake had always wondered just how deep the bond ran between Clem and Cody. So much for Cody the Good. Jake nodded. "I do, Cody. I'm going to hit the hay, but I'll think about what you've said."

"You're stalling," Cody said. "I want Clem out *now.*"

He had to admire Cody's loyalty to his brother. If it was John in trouble, would Jake feel the same dedication to overlook any obstacle to helping his brother? "I can't do that right now, Cody. It's nearly four in the morning. Clem won't suffer for a couple of more hours in jail. It's air-conditioned, and he'll get a meal. There's a doctor who'll check on him periodically. Relax."

Cody shook his head, rose to his feet. "Either you call Rory Whitmore, or I'm going to—"

"Cody!" Erin exclaimed, coming out into the den. "I thought I heard voices! What are you doing here?"

Jake groaned to himself. Cody whipped around to stare at Jake. "Well, well," Cody said, "this is an interesting development."

"Not so much," Jake said. "She was safest here."

He regretted the words the second they left his lips, knowing they'd be like a red flag to Cody.

"My brother had no intention of kidnapping you, Erin," Cody said. "Jake's lying."

"Why would he?" Erin asked. She gave Jake a confused glance.

"Because he just wants you here with him," Cody said. "It's no secret Jake's had a crush on you for ages."

Erin glanced at Jake, her eyes huge. Then she shook her head. "Jake wouldn't have me tied up and tossed into a stall to scare me into letting him protect me, Cody."

"Clem didn't do that," Cody said. "Jake beat him up, so Clem felt like he had to confess something he didn't do."

Erin looked at Jake again. "That doesn't sound quite right, Cody."

Jake stared at Cody. "No. It doesn't. And I don't think anyone else will buy what you're selling, either."

"There's your point of view," Cody said. "And then there's Clem's point of view. You held a man without counsel and roughed him up, which is against the law. If charges get pressed against you, you'll be in big trouble, son, and Sheriff Whitmore even more so."

"Cody!" Erin exclaimed. "What has gotten into you?"

For just a moment, Cody looked guilty. Erin had made many a trip from Farmbluff specifically to check on Cody's "ticker." She'd long kept a faithful eye on one of her most beloved patients, and Cody remembered. It was written all over his face.

Then he said, "Erin, don't you go falling for a man who knows he loves you but will never commit to you. It's a long, dead-end street."

Erin's eyes widened. Jake shook his head. After a moment, Cody went to the door. "You think about what I said, Jake, and you make that call soon. You don't have a legal leg to stand on. And if I were you, I wouldn't want my reputation around the rodeo tarnished. Because if I recall correctly, you brought all your friends to this rodeo. It'd be a shame if they all knew what happened by noon tomorrow, not to mention the sponsors. A man's brand is only as good as his reputation."

He left, slamming the door.

Erin stared at Jake. "What is going on?"

Jake sighed. "Brotherly love, I guess."

Erin looked shell-shocked. "Jake, that part about you having a crush on me for ages—"

Now was not the time to admit it. Erin needed a friend, a safe haven, not a new set of things to add into her life. "Forget about it. You might have noticed Cody was spinning every yarn he could."

She blinked. He let his gaze roam briefly over her, cataloging what he would have liked to spend hours looking at—her tousled hair sparking with chestnut highlights, her soft pouty lips, her tiny feet and slender legs under one of his way-too-long long-sleeved shirts.

"What a night, huh?" she murmured. "My mind is whirling."

"You just need to let me take care of everything," Jake said. Then he scooped her off her feet and carried her down the hall.

Chapter Five

"Now, listen," Erin said, wriggling down from Jake's arms, no matter how much he'd rather she stay in them, "I can take care of myself, buster."

"I know." He retrieved her, carried her into his room, settled her onto his bed. "Don't think I've ever doubted that, Erin." He pulled the covers up over her, to her chin. "You go to sleep now."

Her hand shot out, grabbed him by the wrist. "What did you do to your hand?"

"Nothing," he said, wincing in spite of himself. She hadn't touched his hand, but pain was beginning to radiate up his wrist. "But let's leave our best friend Jake's hand alone, okay?"

She didn't appear amused. The doctor in her took over. Sitting up, she gazed down at his fingers. "You can't even move it."

"It's just a sprain."

"I don't think so," Erin shot back. "Jake Fitzgerald, you've got to stop cutting the details to suit yourself. What happened?"

He sighed, sat on the bed. "I had a small accident."

"Riding?"

"Not exactly." He pushed her back down into the sheets with his good hand. "I've had lots of injuries in my life, and never needed a nurse. So you just stop worrying about me—"

"It's not going to work." Her eyes blazed at him.

"What?"

"Trying to protect me from everything. And by now you should know that I'll eventually find out. This is No Chance, remember?"

He sighed. "True." He rubbed his chin with his left hand. "Tell you what, let's get some sleep now, and we'll discuss this tomorrow sometime when you're not exhausted."

"Me?" Erin looked at him. "One of us is about to fall asleep on their feet, but it's not me, cowboy. You should tell me everything, then go to bed."

He grinned. "Thanks. I was hoping you'd offer." He rolled himself into the bed, crossed his legs and his arms and said, "Wake me when you've got breakfast on," as he closed his eyes.

Erin snuggled down into the sheets three feet away from him, farther away than he wanted her to be, and yet closer than they'd ever been to each other.

"Fat chance," Erin muttered, and Jake smiled to himself.

ERIN KNEW Jake wasn't telling her everything. She had two options: She could allow him to keep protecting her, or she could find out what had really happened. Sheriff Whitmore would tell her.

Jake wanted to protect her, and, while letting a man run her life was unfamiliar to her, Erin realized she'd be taking something away from him that he wanted to give her. Gritting her teeth against her pride and her independence and everything inside her screaming to rely upon herself, Erin decided to let Jake do his manly thing as he saw fit.

At least for one more day. Any longer than that, and she'd probably explode.

On the other hand, Jake taking care of her was kind of sexy. If the circumstances were different, if she didn't feel so much like he was doing it simply because she'd been in danger—and she hated the helpless woman-in-jeopardy role—she'd feel that Jake was quite the old-fashioned romantic.

Until he'd made the crack about her fixing him breakfast. He'd go hungry if he waited on her to serve him…and then she decided that since she couldn't sleep, she'd do just that. She sat up on the edge of the bed—she was surprised by how sound a sleeper he was—and then squealed when he said, "Where are you going?"

Instantly, her pride puffed up. "To the bathroom. Do you mind?" She wasn't about to admit she'd been going to cook him breakfast just as he'd so chauvinistically requested.

"I've got my keys hidden," he murmured, rolling back over.

She hesitated, then got out of bed to walk over and

stare down at him. Poking him with a light finger in the chest, she started when he opened big blue eyes to stare at her. She'd always known he was a sexy devil, but Jake had bedroom eyes for sure.

"Yes?" Jake said. "You were going to gnaw my head off?"

That got her off his sexiness and back onto his pigheadedness. "Yes, I was. Am. Jake, I'm not going to be anybody's prisoner, not Clem's, and not yours."

"Ouch," he said. "The keys are in the drawer next to the stove. Don't be gone too long."

"How do you know I was going someplace?"

"Because I'm out of eggs and you're sweet like that."

Her lips sucked into a shocked pout. Jake's eyes closed, shutting away the lure of the sensual she'd been contemplating, and Erin counted to ten. She reminded herself that this man had saved her from a fate she wouldn't have enjoyed. And he had a broken hand, the big fibbing baby, his right hand. The hand he roped with, poured a simple bowl of cereal with, fed himself with…

She had to go now. She could retrieve her purse and her medical bag from her trunk, then bring back a healthy breakfast for both of them. That's the story she could tell, anyway.

She threw one last glance at the dozing Adonis in the king-size bed and grabbed her clothes.

THE ONLY PLACE open in No Chance at this hour was Ida Lambert's. It wasn't officially open for business, but Mrs. Lambert would be gathering her farm-fresh eggs, milking her cows, and settling a light sprinkling of water over her organic garden of which she was so proud. Mrs. Lambert's was as good as a grocery, if not better, for the items Erin needed.

Not to mention a little woman talk as well. And she had big questions about Cody's claim that Jake had kept a secret crush on her for years. If anybody knew about this, it was Ida.

"Hello!" Ida called, waving to Erin as she pulled into the drive of the small farm on the outskirts of No Chance. Erin loved Dr. and Mrs. Lambert's house. It was like a picture postcard out here—no traffic, no people, just lots of different trees and a white farmhouse cut from the countryside. "Jake called to tell me to keep an eye out for you. He said you were going to fetch him breakfast." Mrs. Lambert beamed, her white apron flapping in the early-morning breeze. "He said you were a soft touch."

The sun rose early in June, but not as early as Ida, Erin thought. No one ever kept anything from her. "He probably doesn't think I can cook."

"I don't think he's particularly worried about his stomach." Ida handed her a basket. "See what my chickens gave me, and I'll rustle up some breakfast for the two of you. How is Jake, by the way?"

She didn't know about Erin's mishap in the arena, or that would have been her first line of questioning. "Thanks," Erin said, "but Ida, I only let you make breakfast if I pay the same amount I'd pay at the Dancing Chicken."

"We'll see about that." Ida grinned at her. "I've got coffee on."

"Thank heaven." Erin went out to gather the eggs, letting herself into Ida's kitchen twenty minutes later. "I don't know how you get so many eggs out of your chickens."

"Free-range. And I sing to them." Ida handed Erin a cup of coffee. "Now tell me all about Jake. I heard he bunged up his hand and isn't riding today."

"He's not?" That was news to Erin.

"He was only riding here for his brother." She stirred some scrambled eggs in a large skillet, poured some pancake batter into another. "Dr. Lambert likes big breakfasts. I don't come home to cook for lunch or dinner. He comes by the Dancing Chicken for snacks, usually."

Erin washed the dishes as Ida cooked. Dr. Lambert didn't go by his wife's restaurant so much for the cooking as to be near his wife. She doubted anyone loved their spouse the way he did his. It was something she'd admired over the years, that steadfast love between two people that never seemed to dull despite life's surprising ups and downs. "Ida, I have something personal to ask you."

"Oh, good," Ida said, "I love girl chitchat."

And Ida wouldn't spill her secret. Despite the town's busybody ways, Erin knew the people who could keep their mouths closed. "Does Jake have a crush on me?"

Ida hesitated in her stirring, then shook her head and went right back to it. "Oh, no, honey. I mean, you two know each other like brother and sister. Jake knew you'd head right over here, for instance. He's always going to keep a protective eye on you. But a crush—" Ida shook her head again. "When there's something between two people, it doesn't usually stay hidden forever. Nothing lives without light."

Disappointment washed over Erin's heart. She'd been hoping, she realized, for a far different answer.

And that's when she knew she was in big trouble. *Because I'm absolutely one-hundred-percent in love with Jake Fitzgerald.*

Or she wouldn't be standing in a farmhouse at the crack of dawn washing dishes and worrying about how he was going to feed himself. She knew very well his hand was hurt because of her. He'd been fine when he'd ridden; he'd been fine when he'd taken her out of the stall. After he'd talked to Clem, he'd injured himself and had to scratch, something he would never have done with two good rides under his belt. He'd taken care of her; now she would take care of him.

"However, I don't mind saying," Ida said, carefully ladling the eggs onto a warming plate, "I rather do think you have quite the crush on our star bull rider, Erin O'Donovan. And I always wondered how long it would take you to realize it."

AFTER ERIN left with two delightfully steaming breakfasts that no man could fail to appreciate, Ida called Sheriff Whitmore. "I'm sending breakfast over for you and Clem and Deputy Gonzalez."

"You're an angel," Rory Whitmore said. "The three of us have been up all night 'cause Clem's got a headache from the thrashing Jake put on him. We've been playing Crazy Eights to try to keep his mind off it."

"I'll be right over with some homeopathy." Ida clucked her sympathy, truly feeling for Clem. "I hope you told Clem that we hadn't planned for Jake to go all ape on him."

"He knows. He's just that anxious to be accepted back into the fold that he's not complaining a bit. But he's smarting, I can tell."

Ida grabbed extra eggs. "Well, I can't go into all the particulars—it's secret girl talk, you know—but tell Clem that our plan is working."

She listened to Rory repeat her words, heard a mutter in the background.

"He says he hopes this plan works better than the one about getting Jake and John to find out about each other."

Ida shook her head. "I'm not going to say that plan hasn't had its rough spots. It would have helped if Marjorie Blaylock could have brought both the boys—Jake and John—back to No Chance when they were born. Still, we've played the hand as best we could, and I think Jake and John are starting to grow on each other. A little, anyway."

"Clem says he's tired of playing the scoundrel."

"But he *is* the scoundrel! Was," Ida amended, heaping some fresh blueberries into a plastic bowl for the three hungry men playing Crazy Eights at the tiny cop station. Men with empty stomachs could get cranky.

"Still, he says if this doesn't work—"

"It will," Ida said. "It already is working."

"How do you know?" Rory asked.

"I know." Ida smiled as she saw Jake's truck, driven by Erin, crest the hill heading back to Jake's place. "The two of them cooped up in Jake's house is great strategic planning. I just wish they had more time alone together."

"I've got an idea," Rory said.

"Make it snappy. I've got to feed Dr. Lambert."

"You go feed the good doctor," Sheriff Whitmore said. "I've got to put a cowboy under house arrest."

"What a lovely idea! By the time you get back, breakfast will be served at the station, so don't stay gone long. And tell Clem we owe him a huge—well, tell him he's doing a fine job." Ida smiled and hung up the phone, then carried a huge platter of food to the best husband a woman could ever have.

JOHN STARED at Jake over the delicious breakfast Erin put in front of them. Jake had called John over to his house, knowing it was time for him to come clean to his brother about a few things. He'd hardly been able to sleep for thinking about what he was keeping from John. Not that he was quite in the same league with Cain, but Jake didn't feel like the world's most heroic brother.

"If I'd known you were eating like this," John said, admiring the plate of steaming food put in front of him, "I would have bought breakfast from Mrs. Lambert every morning."

"It's a town secret. She doesn't want to open the Dancing Chicken early in the morning, but she doesn't like her eggs and whatnot to go to waste. Those of us who know pay dearly for the treat, and she flies under the tourist radar."

"She'd make a bundle. Sit down, Erin. Your food's getting cold, and I'm already eating half your portion." John chewed happily, motioning Erin to sit down and stop hovering. When Erin had returned, she seemed a different person. More nervous, ill-at-ease. Jake slid a glance at her, decided it was the unexpected presence of his brother that had her rattled.

"Remember when you asked me what it was like to have known our parents?" Jake asked, and John stopped chewing.

"Let's forget all that," John said, his gaze wary. "I was new to town. I was weirded out to find out I was adopted and had a twin brother. I'm dealing with everything better now."

Jake shrugged. "Still, it's only fair that you know some things about No Chance. One of the reasons you're not getting much traction with the rodeo is that you're fighting against deep pockets. And history."

"I already know that. The paper-plant guy." John shrugged. "Times are changing."

"Yeah." Jake was beginning to lose his appetite, which was saying something when the breakfast was an Ida Lambert special delivery. "The 'paper-plant guy' is our biological father."

"I think I'll go sit outside on the porch and eat my breakfast," Erin said hurriedly, getting up with her plate. "It's such a lovely morning—"

"Sit," both men commanded, and she did.

"I thought our parents were deceased," John said, a deep frown etching his face.

"Why did you think that?" Jake asked.

"I don't know," John said slowly. "I guess because my adoptive parents are gone…and you never mentioned your—I mean, our—mother and father."

Jake felt guilty as hell about that. "I should have. I'm sorry. They're gone, too. Been about a year or so. I'm sorry I didn't say right off. Bert died of a heart attack and Marjorie just wasn't the same without him. I think she died of a broken heart."

He looked at his brother. "It took me a while to accept you're really my flesh and blood."

They had gotten off to a rough start. Finding out he had a secret twin hadn't brought out the best in him.

"Well," John said, clearly surprised. "I don't know why I didn't ask."

"Yeah, well." Jake shrugged. "You can fill in the blanks on your own. What you thought about me being the lucky twin probably isn't quite the case. I didn't know Gentry Cole was our father when I was growing up and it's a little late for me to care. I probably never would have found out about Gentry if I hadn't moved to Farmbluff. Clem was the one who told me, when we were having our pivotal discussion at the jail."

"My understanding is that Gentry Cole is not all that well-liked. I don't think I've ever heard anybody refer to him as anything other than the paper-plant guy. Or paper-plant jackass, depending on whether there are females present."

Jake waved his hand. "Most everybody calls him that."

"That's a shame," John said. "Everybody loved my parents. I mean, my adoptive mother and father."

"Yeah. Life throws curve balls like that." Jake morosely bit off a piece of toast. "I should have told you sooner. It took me a while to put all the pieces together. Though I'd moved to Farmbluff to try to flush out why No Chance's rodeo was meeting such resistance, I had no thought at all that I had a father who was behind all the trouble."

"He's your sponsor?" John asked, and Jake nodded.

"Once I learned who my real sponsor was, I was pretty ticked. When I was invited to ride for Farmbluff, I figured it would give me an inside look at their rodeo operations. I thought Farmbluff really was my sponsor, just like all of us would be if we hired a cowboy—Dr. and Mrs. Lambert, Sheriff Whitmore, Mr. Pickle, everybody. We'd all vote on it. In Farmbluff, one man pulls the strings."

John shook his head, glanced at Erin. She'd been quiet the whole time, but suddenly she reached over and put a sympathetic hand over John's. Jake was shocked by just how cold his body temperature suddenly went. Cold, as though a river of jealousy poured through his entire body. *I'm jealous. Holy smokes, I'm jealous as hell, of my own brother, who's engaged to a beautiful woman and a good friend of mine. This is not a good sign.*

Someone banged on the door. "Don't tell me you've got another surprise, and you've invited the old man over for breakfast and a happy reunion."

"Hell, no," Jake said, "that'll never happen. It's been like a train station here ever since Erin decided to rent my house from me." He tried to sound light, even sent a wink Erin's way to show that he was teasing, and that he wasn't a bit jealous, but he probably wasn't fooling anyone.

He flung the door open with his uninjured hand. "Good morning, Sheriff! Join us for coffee!"

Sheriff Whitmore entered the room, and nodded at John and Erin. "Good morning, everyone. Sorry to interrupt your breakfast. If my nose doesn't deceive me, that smells like an Ida special." He sighed. "No thanks to the coffee, Jake. I can't stay long. As you know, I've got a prisoner down at the jail to keep an eye on."

"You're working overtime, Sheriff," John said, and Rory nodded.

"It's been a busy couple of days. Worth it, though, if the rodeo is a success," the sheriff replied.

"I believe No Chance will be proud of what it's accomplished," John said. "Next year will be even better, and we'll see what Farmbluff's got up their sleeve in two weeks, but I'd say we hit the ground running and made good time to improve the effort No Chance had already put in place."

"That's great news." Sheriff Whitmore shook his head, his eyes sorrowful. "However, I do have some bad news."

Jake's radar went on alert. "Oh?"

"Jake, you know I consider you a friend, and even more than a friend," Sheriff Whitmore said. "As much as I hate to do this, I'm going to have to put you under house arrest for your assault on Clem the Bad."

Chapter Six

John rose to his feet. "Surely, there's no need for that, Sheriff? Can't this be solved in some other way? Jake was provoked. After all, Erin had been—"

Sheriff Whitmore shrugged his shoulders. "The law is the law, even in a small town. Word gets around about how we handle things. This isn't a time when a wink and a nod can suffice—not that I've ever done that," he said quickly. "Jake, you know my reputation is rock-solid as a fair sheriff."

"I know," Jake murmured. Erin stared at Rory, her face etched with distress. Under no circumstances would Jake allow his problem to become hers.

"There's nothing that can be done?" Jake asked, and the sheriff shook his head. "Well, my house arrest can be elsewhere, can't it? Erin is moving into my house. I've already given her my word."

"Ah, no," Sheriff Whitmore said. "You need to be in your place of residence, the home where you pay taxes and all that."

"I have a house in Farmbluff," Jake said, although

he had every intention of giving it up. He was grasping at every possible straw.

Erin said, "It's okay, Jake. I can find another place to live."

The sheriff put his hat back on. "Well, that's business for the two of you to straighten out. But as far as I can see, this house is plenty big enough, isn't it? Erin, you don't take up much room. Jake, you could use a spot of help with your hand." He raised his palms as if to say *What can I do?* "Everyone would understand if you stayed here together. Besides, I'm hoping we can get this matter cleared up quickly."

"What would clear it up?" John demanded.

"Clem would have to drop charges. Or a court of law would have to find Jake not guilty, of, you know, something of which he's pretty guilty." He smiled. "I'd hire Chloe. She's pretty convincing to juries."

"This could take forever!" Erin exclaimed. "Our court of law meets once a month!"

It was true. Petty grievances that No Chance had could be handled on a monthly basis. Larger matters, such things as murder, would be handled in the city, simply because No Chance didn't have the resources. They hadn't ever had a murder so they'd never tested the system. Jake's particular issue would fall squarely under the petty category.

"Couldn't Jake be released on his own recognizance? Or mine?" John asked. "I can pay bail to the county, whatever's necessary. I'm not familiar with legal matters, but he barely touched Clem.

And we could just as easily bring charges against Clem for his—"

"Now, John," the sheriff said easily. "This isn't the big city. Not every sin can be washed away by crossing a palm with silver. Nice of your brother to try to take care of you, though, don't you think, Jake?"

"Sure." Jake was grateful to John but he was more worried about Erin. He could tell she had no plans to lease his house from him now. She'd find someone else to stay with until she found a house of her own to buy, probably the Lamberts or maybe even the boardinghouse with Mrs. Tucker. "Well, thanks for stopping by, Sheriff," Jake said. "Guess you'll know where to find me for the next month."

"Next two months," Rory said kindly. "As you know, we take the months of July and December off. Bad luck this is June, I suppose."

John cleared his throat and followed the sheriff out with a sympathetic glance at Jake, and an I-tried-my-best expression.

"Don't worry," Erin said quickly. "Jake, neither of us had any idea this would happen. There are lots of places I can stay. I'm like a cat—I can live just about anyplace."

"Yeah, well," Jake said, "I'm more like a dog. I'll be real disappointed if you leave." Then he took her in his arms and kissed her the way he'd always wanted to.

He had nothing to lose.

WILD SPARKS flew. That's all Erin could think, and that there shouldn't be so much static electricity in

June. Jake kept kissing her, and she melted into him, all the while thinking *This is not a good idea.*

Problem was, it *felt* like a good idea. How was a woman supposed to get her mind and her body to think together? She was slipping fast under Jake's spell, helpless to stop it. Eventually, when they finally had to take real, deep breaths, she jumped away, shocked by her response to him.

Her heart was racing. She put a hand over it, realized it wasn't going to slow down immediately. "Jake," she said, "they're doing their thing."

"Who is doing what thing?"

She took a deep breath, measured her words. "Our friends are matchmaking. That's what they do best."

"I'm not exactly opposed. Unless you are."

She was, wasn't she? "I don't know," she said honestly. "All I do know is that I'm not going to fall for this whole line of bull about house arrest and me staying here to take care of your hand. If your hand is in such bad shape, you need to go to a specialist and have it X-rayed and wrapped properly. And get someone here to take care of you. I, for one, am not going to allow our friends to do the same thing Clem was trying to do." She gave him a sad look. "I don't like to be forced to do anything."

He blinked. Stepped back. And she realized in that second what she'd said wasn't at all what she meant. "Jake—"

He shook his head. "I get it. I got carried away."

"Jake—"

His hand went up, stopping her but looking like a gesture of resignation. "Don't feel like you can't stay here, Erin. There's plenty of room—the sheriff's right about that. But I agree with you—under no circumstances will we fall for their plan, if there is one. But just to be safe, we'll be careful not to egg them on."

He disappeared down the hall. She heard a door close. "Oh, lovely," she muttered, "my bedside manner stinks."

But she was pretty sure the right course of action wasn't them cozily playing house together.

"Actually," Chloe said when Erin called her, "Clem pressing charges isn't good. I'd lay low if I was Jake until some hurt feelings blow over."

"This isn't part of the whole get-Jake-back scheme?" Erin glanced down the hall. Jake still hadn't come out of his office. It had been two hours of silence between them.

"No," Chloe said. "I'd say our good intentions have gone awry."

"Can you come get me?" Erin asked. "I need to pick up my car." She didn't want to be dependent on Jake for anything. "I have to find another place to live."

"Don't be in a hurry for that," Chloe said.

"You're on their side!"

"No," Chloe said, "but everybody's busy wrapping up things at the rodeo. I heard a rumor that so much money came in that there'll be enough to offer sponsorships next year."

If Chloe was "hearing" things, she was learning it from John. "What does that have to do with me?"

"John says his corporate buddies were so pleased that they're making plans to rent some houses, whatever they can, and start looking into investing in No Chance. He wants us to buy a few places and rent them out. Prices are going to go crazy around here."

"I'm not in the market for real estate speculation," Erin said. "But I can stay with Mrs. Tucker."

"You could. You could even have John's old room since he's moving in with me after the wedding." Chloe giggled. "But Mrs. Tucker says she's selling her boardinghouse."

Erin's jaw dropped. "Why?"

"Ida Lambert needs help with all the new business she's getting. Mrs. Tucker's going to help her run the restaurant. The more folks visit No Chance, the more chance we have for the tourist trade we were always hoping for. Now it looks like we'll get it. But we'll all have to help each other out. John says we can't go on being haphazard forever."

Erin thought quickly. She needed a clinic and a home. Mrs. Tucker's boardinghouse was quite large, had everything she needed. Or at least could be renovated.

"I can be there in about thirty minutes to take you to get your car," Chloe said.

"Thanks."

"Tell Jake I hope his hand feels better."

Erin glanced down the hall. "I hope it does, too." She wasn't going to be assigned the job of nurse-maid/house sitter for a handsome bull rider who kissed like Prince Charming.

"I'm not so sure you should leave him while he's under house arrest, Erin," Chloe said softly. "If it were me, I'd feel sort of like my good friend was bailing on me in my hour of need. John and I will do our best to get Jake's situation resolved—I know John will move heaven and earth to help Jake—but it'll take a little time. Anyway, I'll be by to get you in a bit."

"Thanks." Erin hung up the phone. She stared down the hall again, thinking over Chloe's words. Deserting Jake in his hour of need was something she'd never do. He'd saved her from heaven-only-knew-what. The sensation of the sack enclosing her, the tape on her mouth, was vivid and chilling. If it hadn't been for Jake, she might be in Mexico right now.

She sat on the sofa and waited for Chloe.

JAKE HEARD the front door close. Peering out a window, he saw Erin jump into Chloe's car. He didn't blame her for leaving. He wouldn't want to be stuck here in this house with him, either.

He wasn't going to be good company.

The whole thing was a crock and a scam. He didn't like going from the town hero that No Chance wanted to the town felon. Was he a felon if he was under arrest?

It didn't matter. He was no longer the "white hat"; he was in Clem the Bad's league. Erin would wash her hands of him as soon as she could.

No. That was selling her short. Erin was loyal to the bone. But he didn't want her feeling sorry for him, staying with him out of pity, and that wrenched his pride the worst.

All he needed to do was talk this over with Clem. The two of them could work it out. This was all Clem's fault, anyway, and even Clem would have to admit that.

Jake walked out into the living room, stared at the sofa where Erin had been sitting not five minutes ago. He liked having her around. Hard as it was to admit, he wanted her to admire him, wanted to be the hero in her eyes. She'd always looked at him with such hero worship.

He needed to talk to Clem.

If he could just get out of here...

Clem wouldn't be eager to help him because the clown would be more eager to help himself. Even though Jake had vouched for Clem to work the No Chance rodeo, the old man had made it clear that his loyalty lay with Farmbluff's rodeo. "I'm an idiot," Jake muttered. "A soft-hearted sucker."

If he could have ridden his last ride, he would have won, he knew it. He'd still be the winner. He felt like a football player on waivers with no season left in him.

There had to be something he could do to change the game.

And that's when it hit him: The only person who could help him was his father.

As much as it would gall him, he'd swallow his pride to ask for help. Anything to get himself back on the road to Erin's heart.

Chapter Seven

Gentry Cole was a big man. He was as tall as Jake and muscular where Jake was whip-cord thin. He had gray hair where Jake's was dark. He watched everything carefully, looking for a moment of weakness.

Jake hated to expose a flank to his father. "I need your help."

Gentry shrugged, made himself more comfortable in Jake's living room. "I got that much. So here I am."

"I'm under house arrest."

"I heard. Good news travels fast. I wish you hadn't chosen to rough up one of my clowns."

Jake gritted his teeth, feeling no connection to this man who shared his own flesh and blood. He felt more kinship with John, though he'd only known him a little over a month. "You and I both know that Clem was up to no good. I want to be released from this trumped-up charge. I want my name cleared."

"You broke your contract with me," Gentry pointed out. "You're leaving Farmbluff in the lurch right before our rodeo. Why should I help you?"

"Because," Jake bit out, not about to play the paternal harp string and say *Because you're my father, damn it.* "Because you don't want me to tell everyone what Clem was going to do to Erin. What *you* were going to do with Erin. What the hell were you thinking?"

Gentry's eyebrows arched. "I have no idea what you're talking about."

"The ranch in Mexico? The sick people who need medical attention? You wanted Erin dragged out there to help them."

Gentry shook his head. "There are no sick people. No one's at my ranch but the people who've always lived there, and believe me, they wouldn't trust an outsider to take care of them."

Jake wondered if his father always managed to look so convincing. "That's what Clem said you had planned."

"Well, it's not true." Gentry sounded genuinely annoyed. "I don't have to waste my time with such pointless exercises, Jake. While I know you don't think much of me, I'm no more ruthless than any other businessman. But I certainly don't have to kidnap a doctor."

"What about the illegal drug trafficking you wanted to cover up?"

Gentry shook his head. "Jake, you have me confused with someone else. Or Clem told you a helluva tale. I'm not happy about his lying, either, and hope you'll keep it to yourself."

"Why would Clem lie?"

"I wonder myself." Gentry frowned. "I pay him well enough."

Something was wrong. His father certainly had him reconsidering Clem's words. "Why would Clem act on his own and blame you?"

"I wish I knew. I always knew he was a disloyal sonofagun, but rumors of drug trafficking is bad stuff." Gentry's frown deepened. "I'm guilty of being a sharp businessman, but not of being a criminal."

"I may have you wrong," Jake said slowly, "all the years of hearing bad things about you may have swayed me."

"Well, No Chance wasn't happy with my business dealings. And they're a soft, tenderhearted bunch. They want to live in the past forever, their heads firmly stuck in the clouds."

That was all true, as much as Jake wouldn't agree out loud with his father.

"You're also a lousy father," Jake said after a long moment. He stared at the man he didn't even know, whom he wouldn't have known if No Chance hadn't been so good at keeping secrets. "You hid out in Farmbluff and never acknowledged me and John."

Gentry shook his head. "What could I do? Marjorie didn't tell me a thing. It wasn't until recently that I learned of what had happened. Apparently, when No Chance decided to get you and John together, they figured I'd never find out. But I did. Still," he said slowly, "I was reluctant to butt into your lives. How much can we say to each other?"

Jake didn't know. He wasn't even sure he believed his father. "You have to have known something. You couldn't have just found out when we did."

"Jake, the people of No Chance live their lives their way, write their own stories. Besides, best as I can recall, you had a good life growing up. I remember seeing you on the ball field. I recall thinking you were a kid with a lot of promise, from a good family doing everything right."

Jake nodded. His mother, Marjorie, and the man who'd raised him—the man he'd believed was his father, Bert Fitzgerald—had made him the center of their universe. Whatever heartbreak Marjorie had suffered by giving John up—and he knew his mother had been tenderhearted like no other—she had kept to herself what must have been a deeply painful secret. But he couldn't remember ever being an unhappy kid. In fact, if anything, growing up in the Fitzgerald household had been idyllic.

If not completely honest.

"What would you have had your mother do differently?" Gentry asked, and Jake couldn't give an answer.

"You have to understand she was young. Eighteen and pregnant. I'd fallen hard for her, but I was from a neighboring town and she had no interest in leaving her family and friends, the place where she'd grown up. I never knew she was pregnant." He shrugged as if it didn't matter, but Jake suspected the gesture itself was telling. His father's pride had been hurt that she hadn't loved him the way he'd loved her. "I never knew I was your father until John Carruth came to town."

"How would that have made a difference?"

"It wouldn't have so much, except that he was setting up to compete against our rodeo. I'm a businessman, I had interests to protect. So naturally I wanted to know who this stranger was and why he would care so much about a piddly rodeo. What makes a billionaire come to No Chance, Texas?"

"Hardly anyone knew John was wealthy."

"All anyone had to do was ask." Gentry smiled at Jake. "In fact, a simple Internet check pulls up his name, his causes, his family. It wasn't too hard to have my sources run a background check on him. Birth records are easy to find. I have to admit it was a shock to find out I was a father." Regret flashed briefly across his face. "I always wanted children."

But Jake was no child now. He figured his mother had done what she had to do, but he wondered how his life might have been different if she'd done the usual thing and married the father of her children.

Gentry laughed softly. "Bert Fitzgerald got himself a helluva deal. Marjorie Blaylock wouldn't have looked twice at him if she hadn't been in a fix."

"Why do you say that?" Jake was suspicious, super-sensitive to any barbs that might be thrown the way of the man who'd raised him, the man he'd always believed was his father.

"Don't go getting all prickly." Gentry waved a dismissive hand. "Bert was no catch. He'd never have dared to ask Marjorie Blaylock, No Chance beauty queen and everybody's best girl, out for so much as a soda."

"She must have seen something in him." They'd been poor, true, but there'd been no lack of love in their household. That had been all that mattered to Jake. His father had never been too busy to be a dad to him. He'd taken him hunting, fishing, taught him how to build things. There wasn't anything Jake didn't know how to do with his hands. He was completely self-reliant, when he had the use of both of his hands. His right hand ached fiercely right now, but he knew he was still self-reliant, thanks to Bert Fitzgerald.

"So," Gentry said, "I'm not sure how I can help you. We're on opposite sides, as far as I can tell." His eyes gave nothing away. "Much as I would publicly acknowledge you as my son, we still have business dealings which have broken down, most likely irretrievably."

"You won't help me because I broke my contract," Jake said flatly.

"Right," Gentry said. "Business is business."

Jake shook his head. "You weren't honest about who was sponsoring me. I had every reason to break that contract."

"I have to do what I can to make sure Farmbluff's rodeo succeeds. Surely by now you've figured out how much this bit of business means to Farmbluff and to No Chance. No Chance certainly did what they could to load their game for success. You can't expect me to do any less for ours. There are folks counting on that employment and the revenues a big-name rodeo will bring to Farmbluff." Gentry looked at him. "I wasn't expecting you to scratch from No Chance's rodeo."

Jake hadn't wanted to. "Believe me, I wouldn't have if there'd been a chance of hanging on."

"Of course you're riding for a town that wasn't being up front with you," Gentry said, his tone silky. "That's your business, of course, but you wouldn't be forced to call me here for help if your No Chance buddies weren't up to their knees in dishonesty."

Jake didn't want to hear that. "What exactly are you saying?"

"This whole house-arrest thing is bogus. You're not wearing a monitor, you haven't been read any rights, have you? No formal charges have been pressed. It's a scam, Jake, courtesy of the 'good' people of No Chance. And isn't this the way they've always operated? In their best interests?"

A little disbelief crept into Jake. "Why would they do that?"

"Not sure. But you're gullible and they used you for whatever it is. Probably just to keep you away from my rodeo. They'll tell themselves it's for your own good. Yet here you are, tied down and thinking you're in big trouble. It's not too hard to read them. I've had years to study their tricks and they're always the same. Smoke and mirrors. Although they did shock me when they pulled you and John out of their hats."

Jake frowned. "It can't all be about the rodeo."

"It's about winning. It's about keeping their lives just the way they want. No Chance will never change. How much luck did John have when he came in here thinking he was going to transform the town into a tourist mecca with his casinos and fancy amusement park attractions?" He waited for Jake to answer. "None," he said, murmuring the word that had been in Jake's mind. "He had all kinds of plans. Everybody was talking about them. But in the end, he caved. Nothing's going to change."

"Are you saying they don't want to grow? Change? Get better? If that's true, why are they fighting so hard for the rodeo?"

"Because," Gentry said with a long look at him, "they're nothing if not a competitive bunch. They only want Farmbluff's rodeo to fail. John was their savior. But they only wanted so much from him. Right now, they've conjured up this whole arrest thing in a last-ditch desperate attempt to control everything. They're using all of us. And I'm aware Clem's got you over a bit of a barrel, but I swear I had nothing to do with it. My hunch is you ask around town for your answers. I'm sorry for what happened to you and to Erin, most especially, but it's none of my doing." He stood, nodded at his son. "I can say it's been a pleasure speaking to you at long last."

The front door opened. Erin, Chloe and John walked in, halting when they saw Jake and Gentry Cole.

"Hi," Jake said, his gaze taking in Erin's blue

eyes, pale face, flame-red hair. He didn't think he'd ever get tired of looking at her. He wished she was his, wished he could make himself an honorable man for her. "John, this is Gentry Cole."

He figured John had done a lot of business dealings with a completely straight poker face, but coming eye-to-eye with the man who was his father seemed to tip John's equilibrium. He said nothing at all, his expression giving nothing away.

"John," Gentry said, putting out his hand. Belatedly, John shook it, remaining silent.

"And you know Erin O'Donovan and Chloe Winters," Jake said.

"Ladies," Gentry said with a nod, "we've met briefly here and there."

"What are you doing here?" Erin asked, blunt as always. Her gaze darted to Jake's. "I mean, this is surely an unexpected surprise."

"No, not exactly." Gentry went to the door. "Jake invited me for a visit. I'll let him fill you in on the details. Jake, I've never known of a contract that couldn't be renegotiated once details change." He nodded at them all and left.

John watched Gentry leave, then turned to Jake. "What the hell just happened?"

Jake sighed. "Just doing what I can to keep my head above water."

"We came to bring you dinner," Chloe said, "but maybe you're not in the mood to eat."

He didn't have a lot of appetite, but he was in the mood for company. "Thanks."

Erin frowned. "I don't understand what happened."

"And I didn't understand why you sneaked off," Jake said. "Erin, I can have guests without you understanding what the visit is about."

She drew back, offended. Jake held back a sigh. He couldn't explain right now, he couldn't even explain everything to himself.

"Hey, I think I'll get Chloe home," John said. "It's been a long day. I'll catch up with you soon."

Chloe went with John to the door, then on impulse turned to hug Jake. "Everything's going to work out."

"I know," Jake said, his gaze on Erin. Would it? He wouldn't bet No Chance's last dime on it.

"I'll call you tomorrow, Erin," Chloe said, and John held the door open so they could leave. After a moment, Erin turned to face Jake.

"Don't keep things from me."

He walked over to her, tipped her chin up with his finger. "Oh, I don't think I'm the one keeping secrets," he said, and then he kissed her, and this time, he kissed her so she wouldn't mistake exactly what he wanted from her.

"Wait," Erin gasped, pulling back from him. "Tell me what's happening!"

He couldn't tell her. He pulled her to him, holding her tight, needing her that much. She was part of him, part of the fabric of No Chance. He still loved her, in spite of what she'd done. But he had to get his good name back.

He wouldn't be riding this time to win a buckle

or money or even her. He'd be riding for his reputation.

And when he took her to his room—her room now—and undressed her, she didn't say anything, not a word of protest. Her body melted against his and she sighed with the kind of longing he'd always prayed he'd hear one day. He took her gently, made love to her like his life depended upon it, because it did.

And in the morning, long before she'd awakened in his big wood-hewn bed, he bandaged his hand, packed his duffel and left before anyone would ever know he'd gone.

House arrest be damned.

Chapter Eight

When Erin woke, she wasn't surprised to find Jake gone. Goodbye had been in his every touch last night. She'd known something was wrong when they'd discovered Gentry there last night. And everything about Jake's determined expression after that had told her that he was leaving.

She didn't blame him. In fact, she completely understood. No man wanted chains put on him, and whether their friends realized it or not, she would have set Jake free herself before watching him wither under the weight of those chains.

She'd gotten her answers from Clem. In the end, it had been that simple. He'd folded like a sheet when she'd told him that she knew he was behind the whole plan of kidnapping her so that Jake would rescue her. She told him she was very, very upset with him, and the rodeo clown had produced a streak of sadness no one would ever have known he possessed. He was desperate for forgiveness, not much different from how anyone would feel after a lifetime of being separated from their family. No black sheep wanted to be black forever, and she hadn't needed those med-school psychology classes to understand what was driving Clem the Bad to suddenly want to be good.

Or Gentry Cole to want to know his sons.

No man was an island forever.

"He's gone," she told the friends she loved at a meeting she'd called at the Dancing Chicken the next night, "I wasn't going to tell you, but you need to know we were wrong. A man like Jake isn't going to be tied to a town or a place just because we want him here." She took a deep breath. "*I* was wrong."

Mr. Pickle, Mrs. Tucker, Dr. and Mrs. Lambert, John Carruth and Chloe and Cody all stared at her in dismay.

"Where did Jake go?" Mr. Pickle demanded.

"Farmbluff is my guess." Erin glanced around the room. "He called his father here for a reason."

"I'll be danged," Cody said. "He's gone over to the dark side of his own volition."

Erin shook her head. "He didn't have a choice. We pushed him there."

Mrs. Lambert looked distressed. "But he's under house arrest."

"He knew we were trying to steal him back home," Erin said softly. "His pride was crushed, his spirit completely stolen from him because we cheated." He hadn't told her any of these words, but she'd read them when he'd held her in his arms last night. Every kiss had been an unspoken surrender. "We were cheating, even if it didn't feel like it at the time. Jake's too honorable for that." She took a deep breath, shaken by what she knew about him now. "He knows everything."

"So now what?" Dr. Lambert asked. Mr. Pickle sat up, his brows beetling.

Erin wasn't sure. "I don't know. We can look at the bright side. Our rodeo was a success, much more than we ever dreamed."

"Thanks to Jake," John reminded them. "He brought in his buddies."

That sat heavily in the room.

"Back to the bright side," Erin said. "We can look to the future now. Chloe and John are getting married, and—"

Ida Lambert burst into sudden tears, surprising everyone. She was such a strong, can-do woman that no one expected this feminine outburst. Mrs. Tucker patted her friend on the back. "We thought we were doing the right thing," Ida said, accepting a lace hanky from Mrs. Tucker. "We were trying to undo some of our past misdeeds. But it's all backfired on us if we've lost Jake forever."

"Now, now," Mr. Pickle said. "There has to be light at the end of every tunnel."

"This tunnel appears to be clogged," Dr. Lambert said, uncharacteristically morose. "In situations like this, it's probably best to stop digging ourselves in with good intentions."

"Aw, hell, now's not the time to second-guess

ourselves," Mr. Pickle said stalwartly. "There's nothing wrong with being proactive planners."

"Busybodies," Ida Lambert said. "We're a Hollywood script for contrivance."

"I don't like the sound of that," Mrs. Tucker said. "I like to think of ourselves as more like angels. Wasn't there a TV show about helpful angels?" She smiled brightly. "Let's see ourselves as good angels."

"Or maybe the A-Team," Mr. Pickle said hopefully. "With me playing George Peppard's role."

"I have an idea," Erin said, "but you probably won't like it."

"That means you'll be Mr. T," Mr. Pickle said. "Go ahead, make my day."

Erin sighed. "That is not what Mr. T was famous for saying, but anyway, my suggestion is that we follow Jake to Farmbluff."

They all stared at her.

"Why?" demanded Dr. Lambert. "This is our home. Our businesses are here. Our lives are here."

"I meant, for the rodeo," Erin said, and they all considered that with frowns.

"Wouldn't that be disloyal?" Mrs. Tucker asked. "To John and all his hard work and all his...money?" Her voice trembled as she spoke, clearly torn between the two brothers.

"Does seem a bit disloyal," Mr. Pickle agreed, glancing at John.

"Don't mind me," John said, "I've got what I want." He squeezed Chloe's shoulders. "I'll go with majority rule here. Whatever the committee decides is fine. I'm just glad you're not plotting against *me*." He smiled, but no one smiled back.

They were all too upset to find humor in the situation. Erin glanced around the long wooden table, seeing long faces and glum postures. "Anybody else got an idea?"

"No," Cody said, "you've always been the ringleader."

"Me?" Erin exclaimed. "I'm a simple town doctor! I've never lead any ring!"

"We did this all because of you," Cody said. "We thought you needed a husband. Of course, we thought it would be John," Cody said, "and I'm still not sure how I ended up losing my daughter in the process—"

"I'll take good care of her, Cody," John said easily, not bothered in the least by his future father-in-law's carping.

Everyone seemed to relax a little at that, except Erin. "I didn't need a husband," she said to the room at large. "If you went to all this trouble to find me a man, you did yourselves a disservice." She swallowed, thinking about how thoroughly Jake had loved her last night. Perhaps she wasn't being quite honest, but they didn't need to know that. "And quit meddling, Cody. I was here when the initial plan was set. Nothing was ever said about finding me a husband. We were all about the rodeo."

Mrs. Lambert waved the hanky. "I won't say we weren't hoping just a teeny bit that you might find a man, Erin. You need one, honey."

Erin's jaw dropped for an instant. "I do *not*." She did, though—she needed Jake.

"Well, we're a bunch of royal screw-ups," Mr. Pickle said. "We can't do anything right. Mr. T wouldn't even be on our team. We're not the A-Team, we're not even the B-Team. We're the C-Team."

"We're the team that cares about each other," John said. "Some teams win all the time and never care about anything but winning. But some teams play together and never win because winning isn't everything."

"That's a first coming from you," Cody said. "I would have thought your competitive streak was as wide as the Grand Canyon."

"It is," John said with a grin. "I'm just trying a different tack with you. There's no point in everybody sitting around feeling as though we failed. We might as well give Erin's idea a shot."

Erin smiled at John but it wasn't a confident smile. "All I'm saying is that we can wait and see what Jake is doing. I'm guessing he'll hope his hand heals and try to ride for his father." She shrugged. "It would make sense."

"But he's ours!" Mrs. Tucker wailed.

There was a murmuring of agreement. Erin nodded. "We want him back, but it's a decision he'll have to make on his own."

"There's nothing we can do?" Dr. Lambert asked with a hopeful glance at John. "Don't we have a sweetener?"

"No more sweeteners," Erin said. "Busybodying

is what's got us into the mess. I put forth that we, as a group, decide to let Jake live his own life."

"That'll be tough," Mr. Pickle said. "We've never let anybody live their own life."

But in the end, that's exactly what they voted to do, except for Cody, who abstained because his brother was still in the jail. Until Clem was out and safe to live in No Chance as one of its beloved citizens, Cody declared, he didn't feel he could vote on anything. His heart just wasn't in it.

That was more "politicking," but Erin was glad to see Cody being loyal, if to no one else but his brother. Something had brought a change between those two; maybe it had been believing Clem was going to be in jail for a long time. No one wanted to be in a jail of any kind. With a heavy heart, Erin went to buy tickets for Farmbluff's rodeo for the entire group. They'd go as a team, they decided, whether it was the A-Team or the C-Team, and they'd let Jake know he had their support, no matter whose side he was on.

Erin knew she'd worry herself sick over his hand. But she'd support Farmbluff's rodeo if Jake was going to. No matter which team he picked in the long run, Erin secretly hoped it would be hers.

Chapter Nine

Jake understood the task ahead of him. He was going to ride for a rodeo that was not his brother's, that was not his hometown's. He was now a hired gun of sorts, just like he'd been before, but this time he was doing it to free himself from what the people he'd loved had done to him.

He couldn't place a single definition on how he felt about what they'd done, but the word betrayed flitted across his mind. Somehow, he felt most *betrayed* by Erin. How much had she been in on the scheme? What had she really wanted?

He'd been willing to give her his house, his money, his heart. For all the years he'd loved her, he had never suspected she had a calculating side.

The whole thing had been a set-up. Gentry stayed out of his hair mostly, for which Jake was glad. He'd just sent a note by way of messenger. All it had said was *Win*.

Jake was thankful that his hand was healing nicely. He was still nursing it along, but he'd ridden with broken bones before. The pain was minor, nothing like the pain in his heart. He was like every broken-hearted country-and-western tune ever sung about girls and guys and not being able to get it right. It was good he was in Farmbluff now, back in the house where he was before, because misery definitely didn't love company.

He'd heard that the No Chance bunch had bought out a box of tickets. Mentally he shrugged. He was sorry he hadn't been able to ride to the end at their rodeo, but Gentry deserved the best he could give him. Gentry had been dishonest, too, right along with the rest of them, but in the end, at least he'd owned up. He'd had his lawyers ready to make sure no charges stuck to Jake and for that Jake was grateful. After all the years of living in No Chance, he was still pretty surprised that he'd fallen for one of their schemes. He should have figured it out right off the bat, but Erin's involvement in it had clouded his normally acute radar. He didn't know if he could forgive her. Maybe no woman could understand what a man's good name meant to him.

Erin should have.

And yet, making love to her nearly made him want to forgive and forget everything. That had been the most magical moment of his life. Everything in him had wanted her to know how much he cared about her. He'd wanted those few moments between them to be special, unforgettable.

Something had told him that they would never have a future together. He thought about his mother and father—Marjorie and Gentry—and decided that possibly some things just didn't work out. Gentry had never married. By the tone of his voice when he'd talked about Marjorie, Jake suspected the young Gentry finding out his love was going to marry another had taken a heavy toll. No wonder he'd turned what some people termed *mean*. But Jake suspected his father was merely protective of his emotions after getting his heart broken.

Maybe he was more like his old man than he'd ever wanted to be.

HOURS BEFORE the rodeo, a limo pulled up in front of Jake's Farmbluff house. He watched from a window as an older gentleman got out of the car. Jake opened the front door to see who'd come calling.

The formally dressed driver didn't smile. "Mr. Cole, he would like to have the honor of your presence for thirty minutes if he could, sir."

"Mr. Cole?" Since when did he send limos after people? "Why didn't he just call?"

"You'll have to ask him, sir."

Jake put his hat on. "I will."

He waved away the driver as he tried to open the car door for him and did it himself. Jake was mildly curious. He'd never wondered where his father lived. *Maybe I'm a shallow person.*

Maybe all I think about is Erin.

They drove a good ten miles out of Farmbluff, going east on country roads that slowly became narrower and less well-marked. The driver turned into a heavily wooded thicket where a small bridge separated a country residence from the road. A big brick mailbox marked the entry, as well as some cattle guards and a gatehouse. The wrought-iron gate moved back and the limo slipped past the gatehouse without stopping. In the distance Jake could see a two-story house, easily eight thousand square feet, built in the Tuscan style. "Pretty far to go out to eat," Jake said to the driver, who nodded at him in the rearview mirror.

At the house, the driver got out and opened Jake's door. Jake climbed out. "I'd hate your job," he said to the driver.

The driver replied, "Sir, I would not like yours, either."

Jake laughed. "Good enough. Where is the old man?"

He was led into the house, into a palatial living room with a massive fireplace and a huge wrought-iron chandelier. The decor was tasteful and expensive, masculine without being all about horns and dead animals. There was the requisite twelve-point buck on one wall, but other than that, there were no other dead things that would give a woman pause. Except perhaps for the leather furniture, but Jake admired the cognac color and expensive feel. It reminded him of the black boots the vendor had been selling in No Chance, the ones with the silver tips everyone had wanted. Fine, hand-tooled leather—was there anything like it?

"You like my furniture," Gentry said, entering the room. "It was made in Italy."

"I wondered if it was local."

Gentry shook his head. "We have fine saddle makers and boot makers here, but this…this I had to have." He ran a hand over the sofa. "It feels like smooth butter."

Jake nodded, done with the niceties. "I've got a ride in a few hours."

"I know." Gentry waved him over to a window. "I wanted to talk to you about something that's been on my mind."

"I'm listening," Jake said, staring at his father up close for the first time. His eyes were the very same as his and John's, a denim blue that stood out against the skin.

"I always wondered, in the beginning, if you were my son. I didn't know about John, of course, because when Marjorie came back from 'visiting,' wherever she'd been sent to give birth, she brought only you back. I imagine it was a tough decision."

Jake swallowed uncomfortably. His life could have been so different. He suspected he wouldn't have fitted into John's lifestyle very well. "I'm glad it worked out the way it did, if one of us had to…" He'd started to say "be adopted" but stopped himself. Why hadn't he realized that Gentry probably wished that Marjorie had come to him? Then both of the boys would have stayed together, grown up side by side, real brothers. Why hadn't that been his first thought? "I'm sorry," he said, "I mean, I had it pretty good growing up in No Chance."

His father looked away. "You know, I came to your games for years, imagining every once in a while that I could see a glimpse of me in you. I was suspicious because you were about the same age as a child…I mean, since Marjorie and I…" Gentry halted, ran a hand through his hair. "Mrs. Branford," he said into a speaker, "could you please bring two snifters of brandy?"

"I'm about to ride," Jake said. "I'll have to take a rain check."

"Yes," Gentry murmured, "this time I get to watch my son."

Jake's throat went tight.

"I'd like to talk to you about my estate in the future," Gentry said, snapping himself back from the past. "I'd like to leave you everything I have. The plant, my property, everything."

Jake blinked. It was the last thing he'd expected to hear. "Why?"

He shrugged. "Why not?"

"What about John?"

"John has my genes in the moneymaking department," Gentry said, his smile thin. "I don't think he needs any more money, do you? I don't think it would be meaningful to him to have an estate in Farmbluff, or a paper plant, or several million more dollars. Besides, I didn't watch him while he was growing up. I never knew about him. You, I wondered about. And somehow, you became more than just the average schoolkid running around on a ball field to me." Gentry took a sip of the brandy Mrs. Branford brought him. "I don't know how to explain it better than that."

"I don't know." Jake shook his head. "I think

you'd be better off leaving whatever you have to charity, Gentry. I'm my own man."

"I know. It's expensive to be one's own man, though."

Jake shook his head. "I'm all right. I'll ride for you—this time—but I need my life to stay pretty much independent."

"Hardheaded?" Gentry smiled at him.

"Something like that."

Gentry nodded. "And Erin?"

Jake pinned his gaze on Gentry. "What about her?"

Gentry's gaze went a bit too innocent. "I might have grandchildren one day, mightn't I?"

"John might be expecting even now," Jake said, determined that his brother wouldn't be left out of the family equation. That was what had bugged him about Gentry's offer, he realized. Maybe John didn't need a father figure in his life and maybe he didn't need any more money, but this man was their flesh and blood and if he wanted to leave provisions for Jake, it needed to be equal between his sons. They were twins, two parts of a whole. Jake didn't want to forget that. Family didn't forget each other, didn't leave each other behind.

"I'll have Doyle take you back," Gentry said. "Good luck."

"Thanks," Jake said. "I'll be wearing the Cole logo proudly."

Gentry's eyes misted. "I've waited a long time to hear those very words."

Jake nodded and left, following Doyle out. "Don't open my door," he said. "Please."

Doyle stood stiffly by. "I must," he said, "it's my job. If I don't do mine, I might end up fired and doing yours and then where would I be?"

Jake grimaced. "Broke and broken, buddy. So do your job."

Doyle opened the door with a discreet grin.

ERIN COULD hardly sit still. "I'm so nervous," she told Chloe, and Chloe nodded.

"Me, too. Good thing you're not working this rodeo."

"I think I'd rather," Erin said. "It's hard being a spectator." Still, the last time she'd worked a rodeo had brought them to this place: All the No Chance gang—including Clem—sitting in one box together as friends at the enemy rodeo. "I suppose it defeats the purpose to support their rodeo," she said glumly. "But I find it hard to care anymore."

"They picked the fight with us," Ida said, and her husband passed her some popcorn. "Ours was better whether they want to admit it or not."

"That's right," Mrs. Tucker said, "and think how much better we'll be next year now that John has some experience under his belt."

John turned to stare at them. Mrs. Tucker blushed. "Not that you did a bad job this year, John."

"At least now I know who's on my side," John said, and Chloe squeezed his hand.

"I'm on your team," she said sweetly, so he kissed her.

"Well," Mr. Pickle said. "How come you and Clem got benched, Cody?"

"Because," Cody said, "Mr. Cole says he can't trust us not to be a distraction." Cody sniffed. "He said we're too old. And he said we're not his clowns anyway."

"You can help at the No Chance rodeo next year," John said kindly, "making balloon animals for the kids."

Cody and Clem had started to perk up and then deflated all at once. Erin would have laughed if she wasn't feeling so antsy about Jake's first ride. "What if he wins?" she asked the group at large.

They all stared at her.

"What if he does?" Ida asked.

"What she really means is, what if Jake decides to stay here and ride for Gentry now that he's discovered all we are is a bunch of schemers, meddlers and nosey birds?" Cody sighed. "I suppose you could get pregnant, Erin. That's all I have left in my arsenal of suggestions."

Many a jaw dropped. "What?" Cody asked with a wag of his white-topped head. "Oh, for heaven's sake, let's all just enjoy the rodeo, if we can."

"She needs a ring to get pregnant, Cody Winters, and you don't suggest otherwise," Mrs. Tucker stated, giving the rodeo clown a slight slap on the arm. "Things haven't changed that much around town."

But they had. All their gazes slid guiltily to John, whose own mother had been pregnant out of wedlock.

"You know," Clem said, determined to be the diplomat for the first time in his life, "this may be a subject best dropped."

"I agree." Dr. Lambert held up some popcorn. "Anybody want any? It's good. It'll keep your mouth shut, too."

They all took a handful.

"I could use some shut-my-mouth popcorn," Cody said. "I guess that's my problem. I haven't eaten enough of that in my life. Erin, my brother and I are sorry for what we did to you. We didn't mean for it to go the way it did. It's like we thought we had our acts together—our rodeo act and the whole Jake-rescues-Erin plot—and the durn thing got away from us like we were boys in our first jeans chasing the calf's tail ribbon."

Erin wrinkled her nose. "That's the hundredth time you've apologized."

"But we still don't feel forgiven," Cody said. "I don't do crime as well as Clem does."

Clem sat straight in his seat. "I don't do crime at all—"

"Look! It's Jake!" Erin exclaimed.

They watched as a bull rushed from the chute. Erin knew Jake's hand couldn't be fully healed. She just knew he had to be taped to the max. And yet somehow he held on.

His score was pretty miserable, for him. She glanced up at the glassed-in box where she knew

Gentry would be sitting. He had to have wanted the Cole name to do better.

"Well, at least he stayed on," John said. "Isn't that the goal?"

"Staying on and scoring high," Chloe said.

"Staying on would be my only goal," John said. "I wouldn't have his job for anything."

"Oh, you'd like it if you tried it," Cody said, and John glanced at him.

"No, I wouldn't. I'm just learning how to ride a horse." John smiled. "I really like my instructor, though."

Chloe blushed. Erin smiled, glanced at the board. Jake was third. If he could hang on to third place... "I don't really want him to win today," she said suddenly. "How's that for a selfish confession?"

They all turned to stare at her again. "I only want him to win at our rodeo."

Ida handed her the popcorn again. "Eat some more of this shut-your-mouth popcorn, Erin, before someone overhears you and tells Jake you didn't want him to win or some other idle gossip."

Erin took the popcorn obediently, but she didn't eat it. She did shut her mouth, mainly because she knew Jake wouldn't care what she thought anymore. He'd already lost faith in her, and Jake was the kind of man who never looked back.

She shouldn't have come. And yet she wanted him to know she was there, hoping her presence would earn her some forgiveness in his heart.

But he hadn't looked their way, even though Ida and Dr. Lambert had held up a sign that read, Jake's Our Homeboy.

And Erin knew she'd lost Jake forever.

Chapter Ten

After his second ride, Jake knew his heart wasn't in it. He wanted to win, but he couldn't stop thinking about Erin. His hand was holding up and his second score was high enough to keep him in third place, but the desire had left him. His normal fire was banked and cold.

He knew Erin was there. Knew the whole gang was there. But he was angry with them. Wondered where the knot of fibs and well-meaning manipulations started and ended. And then his father's surprising offer—admission?—had stunned him. He didn't consider himself a part of anyone's family anymore. The family he'd known and loved was gone.

Except for John. And John was a transplanted Texan now. Jake rewrapped his hand and thought about his new father and his new brother. He was pretty old to get a new family, a real second chance at life. Thirty-two was almost too old to want new people popping up in his life. It brought with it a lot of questions and complexities and strange emotions he'd never experienced.

Jake's few belongings were packed in his truck. He needed time away, far away from No Chance and Farmbluff and all the people pulling his life in different directions. Maybe he'd figure it all out in time. Right now, he planned to do his job.

Then he'd hit the road.

No one could blame him.

"How's the hand?" his brother asked, walking into the stall where Jake was changing his boots.

"Fine." Jake looked at his brother. "Thanks for coming."

"None of us would have missed it."

Jake ignored that. He knew Erin was out there. He didn't plan to discuss her.

"So." John glanced around. "I like it better when you ride for No Chance."

Jake grunted.

"Still," John said, "something tells me you're not planning to ride again for a while."

Jake glanced up, raised his brows. "Mindreading these days?"

"It's a twin thing," John said. "Plus I saw your duffel was pretty full in your truck. Looked like you were planning a trip."

Jake didn't reply to that.

"I mean, who could blame you? If I was you, I'd probably take some time off. Go away, clear my head."

"Thanks for sharing," Jake said. Yet it didn't really bother him that his brother was checking up on him. It should bother him, maybe would have bothered him a few weeks ago. But now it didn't. Their bonds were strengthening, but it had been a long time getting here.

"Hate for you to break Erin's heart," John said, looking extremely pained to have to bring it up.

"Hardly plan to do that," Jake said, going back to changing his gear.

"Yeah, but what we plan and what we do are sometimes two different things. Erin will be hurt if you leave without saying goodbye. We'd all be hurt, but hell, don't take what happened out on Erin."

"I'm not taking anything out on anyone. Erin understands what life on the rodeo circuit is like. And we have no commitment of any kind to each other, except that she's renting my house from me."

"About that," John said. "I don't think she is. Think she'll tell you that if you give her a chance."

"Her choice." Jake refused to get drawn into thinking about Erin. "I've got to get ready."

"Listen, I know I'm probably stepping over the line here but it's been great getting to know you. Finding out I have a brother was a shocker, sure, but since that brother is you," John shrugged, reached for words, "it's a great thing."

"It hasn't been bad," Jake said, thinking about Gentry and the emotion in his eyes. In his heart, he knew Gentry would do the right thing and make both his sons a part of his life. It would take time for them to all come to grips with what they were to each other, but they'd get there.

"I just want you to be happy," John said. "It matters to me. And I think Erin's meant to be part of that happiness. So all I'm saying is…think about it."

"I have."

John took a deep breath. "Okay. Good luck."

"Thanks."

His brother left. Jake watched him go, feeling slightly bad for not being more open, but later on, one day, he'd work on that whole family thing. Right now, he just wanted to move on with his life.

But the idea that Erin's heart might be broken because of him gave his conscience the slightest twinge. Could John be right? Or was it just more of the same brew of No Chance manipulation that he'd drunk before? Jake didn't know if he could stand to find out. It still hurt that Erin had been part of a plot to lure him back to No Chance. As far as he was concerned, people didn't trap each other. They said what they had to say and lived with what came after.

He was prepared to live with the consequences of his actions.

He headed out for his last ride.

"ERIN," John said, taking her by the hand, "come with me."

Erin followed John from the box. "Jake's about to ride, John."

"I know. I think you're better off not seeing it."

"But he could win!"

"He could." John nodded. "Help me jimmy the lock on his truck."

"Wait." Erin pulled John back. "What are we doing now? We said we weren't going to do anymore manipulating."

"You said that. All you No Chance people. I'm just now getting the hang of it. I'm going to get this truck open, and you're going to sit inside it and wait for Jake."

"Why?" Erin's eyes widened. She didn't want any part of a conspiracy involving Jake. "He's still pretty unhappy with me. This seems like a very bad idea."

"He's leaving," John said. "You're going with him."

She stared at John. "How do you know?"

"Brothers know these things. I think some kind of ESP thing kicked in when I learned I had a twin. I seem to know what Jake is thinking. And I know he's heading out."

Erin's heart felt as if it was shattering. She'd been part of chasing him off. "John, I can't do this. If he wants to go, then that's what he's got to do."

"Come on," John said, "this is my first time as a finagler."

"A what?" She watched with some horror as John managed to get the truck door open with some sort of hook thing. "How did you do that?"

"When you're used to unlocking Mercedes and Porsches, a Ford's a piece of cake." John smiled at his handiwork. "And I had a car thief teach me the tricks of the trade in New York. We were giving a seminar on how to avoid getting ripped off, and we hired an ex-con to show us—"

"Never mind," Erin said, shutting the door. "John, you get an A for meddling but I've got to go back in and watch Jake ride."

"Erin, he's leaving," John reminded her. "And a lot of it's because of you."

"I know," she said sadly. "That's just a fact I'll have to accept, isn't it?" She walked away, her heart deeply unhappy. She wasn't going to throw herself at Jake. If he needed time and distance away from her, she'd accept that. She'd waited on him for years—what was a few more?

IN EIGHT SECONDS, he'd be a free man.

He'd walk away from everything for a long, much-needed break. He planned to see the Himalayas. Wanted to go to the top of the Space Needle. Had a hankering to raft through caves in Belize.

All he was going to do was be free.

Jake wrapped his gloved hand tightly in the leather, crammed his hat firmly onto his head and nodded for the chute to open. The bull sprang out and Jake held on for all he was worth. Spinning, leaping under him, twisting, the bull did what nobody else in his life could do: trap him in time. He felt his teeth jar, something pulled under his vest, and the buzzer sounded just as he went airborne.

But he'd made it. Win, lose or draw, he didn't give a damn. He'd done his job.

And it was over.

He didn't even hang around to find out his score, nor how he placed. He changed, accepted some congratulations without hearing them, and then he left, a free man at last.

The man standing at his truck wasn't a welcome sight.

"Nice ride, Jake," Gentry Cole said. "Been thinking about what you said."

"That's good, but I've got someplace to be." Jake tossed his stuff into the back of his truck. "Excuse me."

Gentry put up a hand. "Don't make the same mistake I did."

"I'm not making any mistake. I'm just going to take a small side trip on the road of life." Jake opened his door.

"Erin came by to see me," Gentry said, and Jake stopped.

"Why?"

"She wanted me to know that I'd always be welcome in No Chance. She was afraid that there'd still be some hard feelings." Gentry smiled. "I like a woman who speaks her mind. And who cares about other people."

Jake hesitated. This was all true about Erin. It was one of the things he'd always loved about her. Erin cared about everyone, that's why she was a helluva doctor.

"I got the sense that she's in love with you," Gentry said, "but that could just be my wishful thinking."

"Why would you have wishful thinking?"

"Oh, the usual. I'm human, aren't I? Grandkids come to mind, the requisite matchmaking. You'll understand one day." Gentry turned to go with a rueful smile. "Maybe I'll go suck up to John and Chloe. That's probably where my grandkids will come from."

"Yeah." Jake nodded, glad to hear that his father was going to find an excuse to include his other son in his life.

"It was great watching you," Gentry said, turning back one last time. "Thanks for riding for Cole."

Jake nodded and got in the truck. To be honest, riding for his father had been one of his proudest moments. Bert Fitzgerald had loved watching him ride, too. So had his mother, Marjorie. Finally, it felt like a full circle of family had totally embraced the man he was. For the first time, Jake felt his mother's and Bert's spirits smiling on him. It was good to be a Fitzgerald-Cole—damn good.

"Jake!" Erin ran out to his truck before he could pull out from the parking lot. "You won! You won!"

He hadn't expected that. And he hadn't expected Erin to be so excited for him. He looked at her flushed face, her glowing eyes, her delighted smile. And he wondered about his father's claim that Erin was in love with him. Was she? Was he driving away from the one woman he'd waited for all his life? Even his twin, whom he trusted almost more than anyone, said he'd be making a mistake if he left.

"You won," Erin repeated. She glanced at his duffel in the front seat and his saddle and things carefully packed in the truck bed. "You're *leaving*." Her shoulders slumped.

"I am." Yet he couldn't exactly leave if he'd won—Cole was his sponsor. The winner needed to appear with logos blazing to claim the trophy. It was the right thing to do, it was fair to his father. He got out of the truck, and was shocked when Erin threw her arms around him and kissed him right on the mouth.

She felt great. He wanted more of this kind of winning. "Hey," he said, taking her in his arms, "kisses are for luck before the ride."

"Kisses are for luck after the ride, too," Erin said. "Jake, I haven't kissed you enough."

"I'll say," he said, accepting a few more kisses from her. He felt his anger and resentment wash away. "Would you be kissing me if I'd lost?"

"More," Erin said. "Twice as much. Three times as much."

"Damn," Jake said. "Losing wouldn't hurt near as much." He held her tighter, kissed her deeply.

"Forgive me," she whispered against his mouth.

And he said, "Nothing to forgive."

Her eyes glowed at him. "Let's go get your trophy. And celebrate."

He let her lead him back to the arena. "I had a mind to see the Himalayas," he said, "and maybe a few romantic destinations. You game for that?"

"Are you inviting me for a long ride in your truck?"

"That, and a few other modes of transportation. I'll spring for your travel expenses out of my winnings."

"Hmm," she said, giving him a knowing look. "I'll need to pack."

"Don't pack too much," he said. "At least for nighttime. I'll prefer my personal physician to call on me wearing nothing but her stethoscope."

Erin smiled. Applause broke out when they walked inside the arena. Jake waved to the gang in the No Chance box, and then to his father, who smiled proudly. Holding Erin close against him, he lifted the trophy high and let out an uncharacteristic and triumphant whoop.

He was the luckiest bull rider in the world.

* * * * *

ALEXANDROS KAREDES, SNOW DUSTING the shoulders of his leather jacket and glittering like jewels in his dark hair, stood at the door. Maria felt the blood drain from her head.

"Good evening, Ms. Santos."

His voice was as she remembered it. Deep. Husky. Perfect English, but with the faintest hint of a Greek accent. And cold, as cold as it had been that awful morning she would never forget, when he'd accused her of horrible things, called her terrible names....

"Aren't you going to ask me in?"

She fought for composure. Last time they'd faced each other, they'd been on his turf. Now they were on hers. She was in command here, and that meant everything.

"There's a sign on the door downstairs," she said, her tone every bit as frigid as his. "It says, 'No soliciting or vagrants.'"

His lips drew back in a wolfish grin. "Very amusing."

"What do you want, Prince Alexandros?"

A tight smile eased across his mouth and it killed her that even now, knowing he was a vicious, arrogant man, she couldn't help but notice what a handsome mouth it was. Chiseled. Generous. Beautiful, like the rest of him, which made him living proof that beauty could, indeed, be only skin deep.

"Such formality, Maria. You were hardly so proper the last time we were together."

She knew his choice of words was deliberate. She felt her face heat; she couldn't help that but she damned well didn't have to let him lure her into a verbal sparring match.

"I'll ask you once more, your highness. What do you want?"

"Ask me in and I'll tell you."

"I have no intention of asking you in. Tell me why you're here or don't. It's your choice, just as it will be my choice to shut the door in your face."

He laughed. It infuriated her but she could hardly blame him. He was tall—six two, six three—and though he stood with one shoulder leaning against the door frame, hands tucked casually into the pockets of the jacket, his pose was deceptive. He was strong, with the leanly muscled body of a well-trained athlete.

She remembered his body with painful clarity. The feel of him under her hands. The power of him moving over her. The taste of him on her tongue.

Suddenly, he straightened, his laughter gone. "I have not come this distance to stand in your doorway," he said coldly, "and I am not going to leave until I am ready to do so. I suggest you stand aside and stop behaving like a petulant child."

A petulant child? Was that what he thought? This man who had spent hours making love to her and had then accused her of—of trading her body for profit?

Except it had not been love, it had been sex. And the sooner she got rid of him, the better.

She let go of the doorknob and stepped aside. "You have five minutes."

He strolled past her, bringing cold air and the scent of the night with him. She swung toward him, arms folded. He reached past her, pushed the door closed, then folded his arms, too. She wanted to open the door again but she'd be damned if she was going to get into a who's-in-charge-here argument with him. She was in charge, and he would surely see a tussle over the ground rules as a sign of weakness.

Instead, she looked past him at the big clock above her work table.

"Ten seconds gone," she said briskly. "You're wasting time, your highness."

"What I have to say will take longer than five minutes."

"Then you'll just have to learn to economize. More than five minutes, I'll call the police."

Instantly, his hand was wrapped around her wrist. He tugged her toward him, his dark-chocolate eyes almost black with anger.

"You do that and I'll tell every tabloid shark I can

contact about how Maria Santos tried to buy a five-hundred-thousand-dollar commission by seducing a prince." He smiled thinly. "They'll lap it up."

* * * * *

*What will it take for this billionaire prince
to realize he's falling in love with his mistress…?
Look for
BILLIONAIRE PRINCE, PREGNANT MISTRESS
by Sandra Marton
Available July 2009 from Harlequin Presents®.*

We'll be spotlighting a different series every month
throughout 2009 to celebrate our 60th anniversary.

Look for Harlequin® Presents in July!

TWO CROWNS, TWO ISLANDS, ONE LEGACY

A royal family, torn apart by pride and its lust for
power, reunited by purity and passion

Step into the world of Karedes
beginning this July with

BILLIONAIRE PRINCE, PREGNANT MISTRESS
by
Sandra Marton

Eight volumes to collect and treasure!

REQUEST YOUR FREE BOOKS!

2 FREE NOVELS PLUS 2
FREE GIFTS!

Love, Home & Happiness!

YES! Please send me 2 FREE Harlequin® American Romance® novels and my 2 FREE gifts (gifts are worth about $10). After receiving them, if I don't wish to receive any more books, I can return the shipping statement marked "cancel." If I don't cancel, I will receive 4 brand-new novels every month and be billed just $4.24 per book in the U.S. or $4.99 per book in Canada.* That's a savings of close to 15% off the cover price! It's quite a bargain! Shipping and handling is just 50¢ per book. I understand that accepting the 2 free books and gifts places me under no obligation to buy anything. I can always return a shipment and cancel at any time. Even if I never buy another book from Harlequin, the two free books and gifts are mine to keep forever.

154 HDN EYSE   354 HDN EYSQ

Name _____ (PLEASE PRINT)

Address _____ Apt. #

City _____ State/Prov. _____ Zip/Postal Code

Signature (if under 18, a parent or guardian must sign)

Mail to the **Harlequin Reader Service:**
IN U.S.A.: P.O. Box 1867, Buffalo, NY 14240-1867
IN CANADA: P.O. Box 609, Fort Erie, Ontario L2A 5X3

Not valid to current subscribers of Harlequin® American Romance® books.

Want to try two free books from another line?
Call 1-800-873-8635 or visit www.morefreebooks.com.

* Terms and prices subject to change without notice. Prices do not include applicable taxes. N.Y. residents add applicable sales tax. Canadian residents will be charged applicable provincial taxes and GST. Offer not valid in Quebec. This offer is limited to one order per household. All orders subject to approval. Credit or debit balances in a customer's account(s) may be offset by any other outstanding balance owed by or to the customer. Please allow 4 to 6 weeks for delivery. Offer available while quantities last.

Your Privacy: Harlequin is committed to protecting your privacy. Our Privacy Policy is available online at www.eHarlequin.com or upon request from the Reader Service. From time to time we make our lists of customers available to reputable third parties who may have a product or service of interest to you. If you would prefer we not share your name and address, please check here. ☐

HAR09R

You're invited to join our Tell Harlequin Reader Panel!

By joining our new reader panel you will:

- Receive Harlequin® books—they are FREE and yours to keep with no obligation to purchase anything!
- Participate in fun online surveys
- Exchange opinions and ideas with women just like you
- Have a say in our new book ideas and help us publish the best in women's fiction

In addition, you will have a chance to win great prizes and receive special gifts! See Web site for details. Some conditions apply. Space is limited.

To join, visit us at

www.TellHarlequin.com.

THE BELLES OF TEXAS

They're as strong as the state that raised
them. The Belle sisters aren't afraid to go
after what they want, whether it's reclaiming
their ranch or their family.

Linda Warren
CAITLYN'S PRIZE

Thanks to her deceased father's gambling
debts, Caitlyn Belle's beloved High Five Ranch
is in dire straits. Particularly because the
will stipulates that if the ranch doesn't turn
a profit in six months, it must be sold to
Judd Calhoun—the man Caitlyn jilted
fourteen years ago. And Cait knows Judd has
been waiting a long time for his revenge....

*Look for the first book
in The Belles of Texas miniseries,
on sale in July wherever books are sold.*

From *New York Times*
bestselling authors

CARLA NEGGERS

SUSAN MALLERY
KAREN HARPER

More Than Words:
STORIES OF
STRENGTH

They're your neighbors, your aunts, your sisters and your best friends. They're women across North America committed to changing and enriching lives, one good deed at a time. Three of these exceptional women have been selected as recipients of Harlequin's More Than Words award. And three *New York Times* bestselling authors have kindly offered their creativity to write original short stories inspired by these real-life heroines.

Visit **www.HarlequinMoreThanWords.com**
to find out more, or to nominate
a real-life heroine in your life.

Proceeds from the sale of this book will be reinvested in Harlequin's charitable initiatives.

Available in March 2009 wherever books are sold.

SUPPORTING CAUSES OF CONCERN TO WOMEN ‡‡ HARLEQUIN

WWW.HARLEQUINMORETHANWORDS.COM

PHMTW668

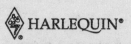

HARLEQUIN®

American ★ Romance®

COMING NEXT MONTH
Available July 14, 2009

#1265 BACHELOR CEO by Michele Dunaway
Men Made in America
When Chase McDaniel learns his position has been usurped by
Miranda Craig, the CEO apparent is stunned. He's devoted his whole life
to the family business—it's his legacy. But the more he gets to know his
gorgeous replacement, the more he wants the job *and* the woman who's
standing in his way. Is there room at the top for both of them?

#1266 A FATHER FOR JESSE by Ann Roth
Fatherhood
Emmy Logan came to Halo Island with her son to make a fresh start. But
what her boy really needs is a man in his life—someone who'll stick around.
Mac Struthers is *not* that man. After raising his two brothers, the last thing he's
looking for is another family. So why is the rugged contractor acting as if that's
exactly what he wants?

#1267 LAST RESORT: MARRIAGE by Pamela Stone
Charlotte Harrington needs to get married—quickly! With her grandfather
looking at every move she makes managing one of his hotels and a slimy
ex-boyfriend on the scene, Charlotte is desperate. And a fake marriage with
playboy Aaron Brody seems a harmless way to buy her some time—until she
falls in love with him.

#1268 THE DADDY AUDITION by Cindi Myers
Tanya Bledso has returned to Crested Butte to raise her daughter and run the
local community theater. She expected to find the same quiet, quirky small
town—but the place is bustling! And it's Jack Crenshaw who's responsible for
this mess. Tanya will tell her former high school sweetheart what she thinks of
his *development*…as soon as she conquers the attraction between them!

www.eHarlequin.com

HARCNMBPA0609